BURNT FUR

EDITED BY KEN MACGREGOR

Copyright © 2020 by Blood Bound Books

All rights reserved

ISBN: 978-1-940250-42-7

Cover by K. Trap Jones

Interior Layout by Lori Michelle
    www.theauthorsalley.com

Printed in the United States of America

First Edition

Visit us on the web at:
www.bloodboundbooks.net

ALSO FROM
BLOOD BOUND BOOKS:

TABLE OF CONTENTS

THE MOON IN HER EYES

SARAH HANS

NIGHT IN THE FOREST is dense and close, and smells of green things growing and the creep of shadows. My thoughts are consumed with the rabbit I'm hunting when I catch the scent of sunshine and peppermints. I pull up short, letting my prey scamper off into the ferns. I raise my head and breathe deep: sunshine and peppermints and the warm vanilla smell of human skin. My fur prickles and my hackles raise. There's a human in my woods.

I find her easily enough. She's not yet a teenager, just on the cusp of puberty, and she huddles in the hollow beneath an oak tree—*my* hollow in *my* oak tree—and shivers so violently I can hear her teeth clicking. A twig snaps beneath my paw as I approach and her breath catches. The scent of adrenaline rolls off her skin, hot and tangy. She's afraid, and rightfully so. I might be old and blind, but these are still my woods. I am still a wolf.

We're near the border of my territory, here, closer than I generally like to be. Not a hundred yards from the hollowed oak, the trees and ferns give way to the velvety grass of neatly trimmed lawns. There's a loud bang, a screen door slamming, followed by heavy footsteps. I crouch defensively and the girl whimpers. The footsteps make their way across the nearest yard and crunch into the dead leaves at the edge of the forest. The combined odors of skunky beer and human sweat reach me and curl my lip.

"Hannah?" The man calls in a voice deep and gravelly. "Where you at? It's not safe in the woods alone at night, girl. Don't be stupid."

The girl holds her breath. She's silent as a rabbit hiding in a thicket.

The man calls for her a few more times, belches, scratches himself. "Fine, then, stupid brat. Stay out here all night for all I care." He turns and goes back to the house, footsteps unsteady in the darkness, tripping on the porch steps and cursing, slamming the screen door.

The girl breathes again. She shifts in the hollow, scuffling her feet against the leaves, curling up into a ball. She sniffles and whimpers for a short time. Eventually her breathing slows as she falls asleep.

I hide myself a few yards from the oak and spend my night crouched among the ferns. When I wake at first light, the girl is gone.

***

My belly pinched with hunger, I find the clothes I keep stashed in a trash bag buried in a shallow grave. I go into civilization with my cardboard sign in one hand and an old coffee cup in the other, camping out in front of the strip mall on the edge of town. Enforcement of anti-panhandling laws here is lax and the landlord is sympathetic to my plight. Most people ignore me or drop a few coins into my cup. A few mutter about calling the cops. A man who smells like freshly mown grass brings me a cup of coffee and a breakfast sandwich wrapped in crisp paper. The food tastes like chemicals, like metal machines and rubber-gloved hands, but I eat it anyway.

Once upon a time I was too proud to beg, and too proud to eat food I hadn't caught myself. Those times are long past, eroded along with the forest, developed into housing complexes and apartment buildings. Game is sparse now, limited mainly to small birds and fat squirrels and the occasional rabbit. I have to supplement my diet somehow, and my self-respect is not so low that I'll stoop to dumpster-diving quite yet.

You might wonder why I don't attack the humans who invade my territory if I'm so desperate for fresh meat. Don't flatter yourselves. Humans like to think they're some kind of delicacy, but, if you are what you eat, your kind are made of sugary drinks and preservatives and the inedible parts of animals rendered with chemicals and pressed into entertaining shapes. I'd rather eat garbage.

It's much easier to eat on your dime than it is to gnaw on your bones. By lunchtime I've collected a fair bit of change and I'm thinking about hitting up the sandwich place across the street with whatever I have. Then the scent of sunshine and peppermints hits me and I'm frozen in place. Multiple footsteps approach: two people; no, three. The girl is accompanied by the man—even under the liberal application of pine-scented aftershave I can detect the odors of sweat and beer oozing from his pores. There's a woman with them, also, a woman who is so quiet her footsteps barely register under the footsteps of the other two. She smells faintly of lavender, but otherwise she's invisible to my senses.

The man growls something about lazy beggars. My skin prickles, rage tingling behind my breastbone.

"Why does she have the moon in her eyes?" The girl asks. She thinks she's whispering low enough for me not to hear her, but of course I'm blessed with the hearing of the blind and the hearing of the wolf.

"She has cataracts," the woman replies. Her voice is small and soft. "Remember, your Nana Drummond had them? She got an operation to have them removed before they were very bad."

"She should've taken care of them before they were irreversible," the man says, not bothering to lower his voice. Now that he's closer I can smell the cancer on his breath. He doesn't smoke anymore, but he did, for too long, and his death is closer than he realizes.

The scent of peppermints grows stronger as the girl approaches me. "Hello," she says.

I blink at her in surprise.

"Hannah, get back here," the man orders.

"I want to give her money," Hannah says, and I can picture her chin jutting out defiantly.

"Not my money, you're not."

I know that tone: it's a warning of impending violence. I should walk away, and fast, but I find myself rooted in place.

"It's not your money," Hannah says. "It's my money. I earned it walking dogs, and I can spend it on whatever I want."

"Clark, let her do something nice with it if that's what she wants," the woman says in her small voice. "She's trying to do something good."

"Shut up, Barb. She's trying to do something *stupid*."

THE MOON IN HER EYES

With the quiet shuffle of old, soft paper, Hannah drops bills into my cup. I don't know how many, but it's probably ten or twenty dollars, depending on the value of the bills. "I'm sorry you have to beg for money. I hope this helps," she says in a whisper.

I nod and muster a smile. It feels unfamiliar and strange.

Clark is on top of us in a rush of heat and swearing. He pulls Hannah away from me. She screams, short and shrill, calling for her mother and stumbling down the sidewalk toward Barb. I snatch the bills from the cup and shove them in my pocket. Clark grabs my arm. "Give that back."

I bare my teeth and snarl at him. I can't see his face, but I can feel how his body reacts to the sound, tensing with fear, releasing endorphins, preparing to fight or flee.

The bells on the nearby restaurant door jingle and the peppermint and lavender odors retreat in a rush of hamburger-scented air.

"You're crazy. You're not even worth it," Clark says through gritted teeth. His breath on my face is rank.

I realize then we're gathering a crowd of onlookers. Not many, but a few. They keep their distance, but they're obviously concerned. Even without vision I can sense their alertness, the tense posture of their bodies and the quickness of their breathing. "Hey man," someone says. "Let go of her. She's just an old lady. She's *blind*, man."

No one approaches, but Clark isn't stupid. Violent, dangerous, but not stupid. He's not going to hit an old woman in public in front of witnesses. I suspect he only hits his wife and daughter when he's sure nobody else is around. What a big, tough man he is; so unafraid to hit a defenseless woman.

Of course, I'm not defenseless. I'm just as dangerous as he is, even without a wolf's powerful jaws. I drop my cardboard sign and my hand finds the knife in my pocket, the one I've carried for years, because I'm not stupid either. As Clark lets go of my arm and steps away from me, however, I find myself glad I don't have to use it.

"Don't let me see you here again," he says over his shoulder as he strides away.

Once his pine-beer stink has retreated, the onlookers retreat as well. Someone presses a wad of bills into my hand, murmuring something polite. I wait until I'm alone before slinking back into the forest.

***

My clothes once again buried, I shed my human guise to become a creature of fangs and fur. There was a time when the wolf-pelt was the one that felt like a disguise, but that was long ago, before I became a full-time resident of the forest.

I catch a chipmunk and gobble it down, fur and bones and all, barely tasting it. Then I nap for a while in the ferns near Hannah's house. I wake licking my chops, roused by the delectable odor of charred meat. I'm up and moving toward the scent before I'm even fully conscious. I know it's evening by the temperature, the fern fronds chilly as they brush my flanks.

Halting at the edge of the forest, I crouch in the dead leaves and listen. Clark mans the grill. He's drunk, the reek of bourbon searing my whiskers. He gives commands to Barb and Hannah, who obey with alacrity, stinking of fear.

Hannah doesn't bring him the bratwurst quickly enough and he swats her. She hits the ground. A growl burbles up in my throat and I swallow it. Hannah flees for the house and Clark follows, bellowing. The grill is unguarded while he screams at his wife and daughter in the kitchen. There's a sound of something crashing, Barb's voice, the thump of footsteps.

I make for the grill, pulling a bratwurst off the heat and swallowing it in one bite. I snatch another one and run for the trees, where I take my time enjoying it. When I'm done, Clark is still in the house, though I can't hear any fighting. The grill still smells like meat: steak, specifically. My favorite, and no doubt intended for Clark.

I'm full, two bratwurst more than enough food for my starved belly, but I can't resist the temptation. I run to the grill and grab the steak in my jaws. My mouth fills with hot, delicious beef flavor.

The screen door slams and I freeze. Someone gasps, and I can tell by the timbre of the voice that it's Hannah. Her breathing is rapid, staccato, her heartbeat hammering. She's probably never seen a wolf up this close before, with only a few feet of lawn separating us, no fence or wall or pit to keep her safe from the predator.

On those rare occasions that humans see my wolf, it always feels wrong, like a forbidden secret revealed, like the most intimate part of me exposed. Hannah doesn't move or speak for long, breathless seconds, as if she, too, realizes the gravity of the moment.

Then Hannah licks her lips and whispers something. I don't hear it the first time over the rush of blood in my own ears, but then she clears her throat and says it louder. "Take it."

Clutching the steak in my jaws, I dip my head in acknowledgement and then make for the forest at a trot.

***

Hannah visits the forest again in the wee hours. She huddles in the hollow oak for a long time, sobbing, before she finally calms and falls asleep. I wait near the tree all night. I'm the only predator in these woods, but that doesn't mean the girl's safe. Clark doesn't chase after her this time, however, and in the morning she trundles back to the house.

I spend my day napping and eating chipmunks. That evening, Clark grills steak again, but this time he sits in a lawn chair near the grill, the delicate fabric and metal frame of the chair creaking under his weight. He swigs bourbon directly from the bottle. The combined scents of metal, oil, and gunpowder tell me there's a firearm in his lap, so I don't attempt to steal any meat, though my mouth waters. He eats the steak in his chair instead of going inside, as if taunting me.

Thunder grumbles as dusk settles over the neighborhood. Clark closes the grill and goes inside as the first fat raindrops fall. I retreat to the hollow oak and drift asleep to the patter of rain on the ferns.

The scent of peppermints, sunshine and vanilla wakes me. A hand touches my fur. Hannah lets out a startled scream and backs away from the hollow, slipping on the wet earth and sliding to the ground.

I follow her out into the rain. She struggles to rise in the dark and the mud, sobbing and shrieking. Even with rain pounding down around us, her noises will attract attention if she doesn't hush.

Giving up the last scrap of my dignity, I approach her and lick her face like a dog.

Hannah screams, but then quiets. I can feel her staring at me, so I let my tongue loll from my mouth. I'd try to make puppydog eyes at her, but that's difficult to do in the dark, with lenses blinded by a milky white film. After a few moments I lower myself back to the ground and nudge her hand with my snout. She makes a perplexed sound but strokes my wet fur.

I move toward the hollow and she follows, sniffling all the way. Together we climb beneath the oak and together we huddle against each other for warmth. Hannah shivers for many minutes, her teeth chattering, but eventually her trembling subsides. She curls up beside me and falls asleep, her fingers tangled in my fur.

Sometime during the night, the thunderstorm moves on. The sound of falling water is replaced by the chirping of crickets and the soft rustle of bat wings overhead. The forest's usual sounds are interrupted by booted footsteps and rasping breaths. I lift my head and scent the air: Clark is here, with his stink of alcohol and charred meat and cancer.

Hannah stirs beside me. She sucks in a breath as if she's about to speak, but then she hears the footsteps, the careless crash of boots on broken branches. She gasps and throws her arms around my neck, engulfing me in warm vanilla.

Clark stumbles toward the oak. I crouch low, a growl rolling in my chest.

"Hannah!" He shouts, his speech slurred. "Come out this minute. Your mother's worried 'bout you."

Hannah's fingers clutch at my fur reflexively, little pinpricks of pain blossoming on my skin where she tugs the strands. She buries her face in my side.

I catch a whiff of the gun, then. The fresh gunpowder is like pepper on the back of my tongue, acrid and burning.

"Hannah," he calls again. He staggers away from the tree.

"Clark, come back inside." A high, quavering voice and the scent of lavender.

Hannah's fingers release me, and she starts for the mouth of the hollow. I move to block her with my body.

"It's late and it's dark," Barb reasons. "Come inside before it starts raining again."

"I told you to wait in the house," Clark snarls. "I'm not leaving my daughter out here with a wolf on the prowl, even if she is a stupid brat."

"She probably just went to a neighbor's house. Come back in, and put the gun away, and we'll make some calls."

THE MOON IN HER EYES

"'Put the gun away?' This gun is the only thing standing between you and that wolf, woman! How dare you order me to do anything? You're not the boss around here, I am!" Three quick strides and he closes the distance between them.

"Of course, of course you're the boss, Clark, I just thought—"

Barb yelps as he strikes her. "And there's your whole problem. You should let me do the thinking. You ain't too bright, you know that."

Hannah pushes at me and groans pitifully, but I hold my ground.

"Yes, yes, of course Clark. I'm sorry," Barb says from below him. The hit must've knocked her off her feet.

Clark moves away from her and toward the forest again, calling for Hannah. He pumps the shotgun, and I hear the rasp of fingers grabbing fabric. He shouts, "Woman, why're you still here? Get back in the house!"

"Please, Clark, please. Don't hurt my baby girl." Barb must be clutching at his clothes in desperation.

Clark shoves her away. "I told you I'm the boss here." And then his words are reduced to incoherent shouting as he strikes Barb again, and then again.

Hannah wails, pushing past me with panic-strong arms, and runs out of the hollow. "Stop! Mama!"

Clark stops hitting his wife. "Hannah? You stupid girl. Look what you made me do."

Barb gurgles wetly. Hannah runs to her but ends up tussling with Clark. I can't see the fight, but I can hear it, grunts and whimpers, Hannah crying "No!"

She kicks him in the stomach; I know from the sudden *whuff* of air from his lungs. He wheezes, no doubt doubled over with pain. Hannah scrambles across the slick ferns to her mother and lets out a long, low sob that raises every hair on my furry pelt.

I dash to her side, keeping close to the trees and ducking under ferns.

"I'm sorry, baby," Barb sighs. She gives a long, rattling, wheezing breath and grows quiet.

Hannah screams and screams. Clark staggers over to them. I hear the intake of breath as he draws back the gun.

Mustering every bit of strength in my old bones, I tackle him to the dirt. The gun flies from his hand and I hear it strike a tree nearby.

All the air is knocked from his lungs when he hits the ground, and he gasps like a fish under me, flailing. He throws me off his chest and sends me spinning through the air.

I land hard, wriggling to my feet and scampering off into the brush before he can rise.

Hannah stands just as the rain starts again. I can hear her breathing hard and squelching through the mud toward her father. She doesn't help him to his feet, but rather casts about the ground looking for something.

The gun is easy for me to find, even in the rain. It smells wrong in the forest, a thing made of metal. I stand over it and let out a short, sharp howl that sounds almost like a dog's bark.

"Thank you, wolf," Hannah says, her hand brushing my ears as she bends to lift the weapon. I wonder whether she knows how to use it, but my question is answered when she hefts it to her shoulder and pumps it decisively.

Clark struggles to his feet, rasping. The cancer smell intensifies. "Hannah, bring me the shotgun," he gasps.

"You killed Mama," Hannah says through gritted teeth. "I'm gonna give you exactly what you deserve."

The gunshot is deafening. I can't see what's happening, and now I can't hear much either. When the ringing clears enough for me to hear again, the two of them are grunting, and there's the sound of feet squelching in mud and the slap of flesh hitting flesh.

"Give me the damn gun," Clark orders. "You don't know what you're doing with that thing."

"You bastard! You killed her!"

Thunder crackles and lightning zips across the sky. My vision is bright white for a split second, and I can see the hazy, gray silhouettes of a slender teenage girl and a huge man struggling over a shotgun. She lets go, and he staggers back to fall over in the mud.

Darkness closes over us again. I follow Hannah as she runs back to the house, keeping to the bushes that edge the yard. She opens the screen door and fumbles with the knob for the interior door. She makes a discouraged moan when the door doesn't open.

Clark staggers out of the trees. He laughs and I hear the jingle of house keys as he mocks his daughter. Of course he locked her out. He wouldn't want her sneaking back into the house while he's out here looking for her. He squelches up the lawn toward us. "Where's your dog friend now, eh?"

With a desperate, strangled war-cry, Hannah rushes her father, driving them both to the ground. I bound after her and follow the stench of booze and cancer to land on Clark's chest. This time, I don't give him a chance to throw me off. I open my jaws and place them around his neck. I let him feel the sharp points of my teeth, let him know how much self-control I'm choosing to exercise. He freezes beneath me, going stiff with terror.

Hannah gains her feet and stands over us, breathing hard in the rain. I wait while she decides. She speaks softly, first, so I can't hear it under the drumming of my own heartbeat and Clark's, and then she shouts with a guttural growl: "Do it. DO IT."

Clark thrashes but it's too late. I bite down hard, latching onto his neck. Hot blood spurts into my mouth as I rip out his windpipe. Spitting out the chunk of flesh, I back away. He gurgles and flails. His death throes are over quickly.

The rain washes the vile taste of human blood from my mouth. I trot over to Hannah, who sobs and shivers. I press my head against her hand.

"What will I do now, wolf?" she whimpers, stroking my fur.

I lick her palm, and then look up at her. Lightning courses across the sky again and Hannah issues a little gasp. "You have the moon in your eyes."

Nuzzling her arm, I open my mouth and close it gently over her hand. I let her feel the sharp points of my teeth, as I did her father, but again, I wait while she decides. The last bite changed her life, and so will this one.

She stares off into the woods for a few long moments before turning back to me.

"Do it," she whispers.

Moments later, her hand bearing a few fresh puncture marks where my teeth pierced her flesh, we walk into the forest together. When the rain stops and I sense the moon peeking through the clouds, I throw my head back and howl. Hannah follows suit, her human voice becoming richer and darker until it's the voice of the wolf. Sheathed in fur, we make our way into the heart of the forest. My forest. Our forest.

MALLARD'S MAZE

JOSEPH SALE

For Ducky, my first love

IT'S MIDNIGHT; PHAEDRA SITS by the lake: the one on the university campus, the one the students pile into every year around graduation, butt-naked and screaming horny, in some form of ritual annihilation. The lake is calmer now, save for the ducks. They are in mating season, and also horny as fuck. She watches as two green and yellow males chase a speckled, downy female. One of the males turns on the other, quacking like a machine gun on burst fire. Eventually, the second gives up pursuit.

Returning his attention to the female, the mallard cuts over the water like a fighter jet. Hers is the game of endurance. Taking to the sky, looping around. Dancing, whirling. But he is tireless. Eventually, he snatches her out of the air. The two plummet, a feathered comet. As they crash into the water, the male squawks in triumph. He holds the female's head under the water with the violence of his mating. When it is done, the female is dead. He has drowned his mate during the act.

Did you know a male duck is called a 'drake'.

Did you know there are instances of homosexual necrophilia amongst drakes?

Phaedra fucking hates ducks.

Once, her Secondary School biology teacher, Miss Esmer Powell, told her that 'ducks are the most perfect sexual specimens'. Perfectly vile, Phaedra thought. It was about the one thing she'd disagreed on with Miss Powell. She was a wonderful teacher, if a little on the edge sometimes of what was appropriate for students aged nine to ten. She got away with it because she was as charismatic as she was authoritative. As pretty as she was tactful. And her knowledge of wildlife, flora and fauna, species of animal, was frankly mind-blowing. Phaedra had been amazed to discover she didn't have a PhD. It was part of the reason Phaedra was on a mission to get one herself.

She needed a woman like Miss Powell in her life right now. Her last partner: a fucking joke. Lazy, entitled, all the usual symptoms of a fucking god-awful upbringing. She wondered what'd attracted her to him in the first place. It was hard to remember. Before then, quiet Jen. Jen had been a cutie, no mistake. Too cute. Turned out she was too pretty for just one lover. When Phaedra confronted her, she played the polyamorous card. Well, that hadn't been on the table when they first got together. *Thanks for keeping me in the loop, fuckhead.*

Phaedra put her head in her hands.

She was icy cold and not dressed for it. She'd thrown on her best navy blue dress, a figure-hugging one-piece with a low back designed to draw eyes. The sounds of the city were strangely distant. Though the university campus was near the town centre, the student accommodation and hills seemed to wall off the sound. It was like being in a totally different city, which is why she'd come here, to get away from the thud of classless bars and desperate men.

The ducks continue to glide and flit back and forth across the waters, drawing patterns, scar-like ripples. A moorhen, a prehistoric looking thing with raptor claws, pads out of the long rushes and peeks curiously at her.

'Yeah, I'm wearing my plumage today, but there are no fucking decent mates out there.'

The moorhen cocks its head.

'I know, I know; I should just be patient, wait for Mrs Right.' She pauses. She was going to add *Or Mr Right,* but she has a funny feeling it's not going to be a *him.*

The moorhen makes a noise, pads off into the dark.

She follows it with her gaze, as far as she can. She should probably set off home soon. Her flat isn't far, just on the other side of town. It's a route she's walked and jogged countless times: down the High Street, left on London Road, up the hill towards Edgar Mount past the redundant train station, Old Bill, then finally over the hill and right onto Maggy's Lane. There endeth the pilgrimage.

Something catches her eye. A glint. Perhaps it's the moonlight catching something, like a necklace, or a ring. But it's now not so much the light, the brief speck, that enthrals her. It's the shadow beside it. Someone is on the other side of the lake.

She hears a murmuring of voices, then louder:

Get away. Put that fucking thing away. Take it off. Get away.

Phaedra is frozen to the park bench, her ass glued to the cold, cold metal. She feels like if she moves, something will leap out of the dark and cut her down.

Call the cops, she thinks. *Just fucking call the cops.*

A scream, cut short. She now knows what the flash is. It's a knife, a butcher's knife like something out of a fucking eighties horror flick. The shadow moves, transmogrified. It has turned around. She sees the bloody knife now clear as day, floating in the hands of the shadow, like something from *Macbeth. Is this a dagger which I see before me?*

Yes it fucking is and it's fucking shit-scary.

The shadow is dragging something behind it, a corpse. It's a young woman in ass-hugging jeans and a tank top, can't be older than twenty. She's dead, very, very, very much dead. The killer lays her down on the marshy banks of the lake, begins to undo her clothes. Phaedra cannot watch anymore. She turns and takes out her phone.

'999, what's your emergency?'

As the operator on the other end of the line starts talking, Phaedra walks away, stealthy as she can. She already took off her heels to sit on the bench and she leaves them behind. She's blonde, with shiny ringletted hair, but unlike movie-blondes, who couldn't open a can if you gave them a can-opener, Phaedra's smart. She's not hanging around.

'Yes, hello. Someone's been killed.'

'What? Oh shit. That sounds . . . Wait one second.'

'Yes! A girl, in the uni park, she was stabbed—'

Phaedra turns and gets a flash of something that almost gives her a heart attack then and there. She starts running, before she even knows where she is going, before she even knows whether she is sure she has seen what she has seen.

The killer is *sprinting* towards her. None of this Mike Myers slow-walk. He's running full pelt, knife gleaming.

The worst thing of all is Phaedra is sure, *so sure,* that he is wearing a duck mask.

***

As she breaks out into the light of the High Street, she's never been so glad to see an All Bar One. It's a fucking dirty place, and salsa night tonight, where everyone uses a few cheap cocktails as an excuse to grind all over each other, body-odour and all. But it's light, civilisation, *other people.*

As she looks behind her, along the little dirt path leading into the university campus and park, there is no sign of a killer, loitering, running, or otherwise. Fuck, did she just hallucinate the whole thing, did someone roofie her?

She checks her phone. Cops have hung up. She tries to call them back, but the line is engaged. *Shit.* She decides she needs a jolt of sanity. She does the thing you're never supposed to do *ever,* let alone when you're drunk and scared there might just be a fucking lunatic on the loose. She decides to call her ex.

Tim picks up on the second ring. Phaedra is now marching down the High Street, the cobbles giving her bare feet a bit of trouble, but she is glad to be back in the thick of reality. She even doesn't mind the catcalls from a bunch of chavy twats that look like knock-off, shittier versions of the guys from Made in Chelsea. Not tonight.

'Phaed, why're you calling?'

Two things she hates in one. No hello, how are you, or etiquette of any kind. Second, that fucking nickname, the one that makes her sound like a ghost. Due to her pale skin, she got a lot of shit at school, got called Milky, Ghosty, Dead Girl Walking, and all kinds of horrible shit. 'Phaed'/'Fade' reminds her of that.

'Look, I just, I don't know why I called. I just needed to talk to someone. It's been a weird night.'

'Yeah?'

'Yeah.'

All at once, she remembers what she first liked about Tim. He can pretty much accept anything you tell him. Of course, it means he has no opinion, but it's fucking great when you just need to download.

'Thought I saw something pretty fucked up . . . '

As she talks, a police car hurtles past, sirens blazing.

She follows it with her eyes. She half expects to see the killer, standing in the street, waiting for the car with knife-upraised.

'Like what?'

'A crime, or something.'

She stops, bends over, throws up on the street.

'Jesus, Phaed. Gross.'

'Sorry,' she whimpers. 'Sorry.'

'You sound hammered to me. Just go home, have a pint of water, sleep it off.'

'I'm not drunk.'

'I gotta go, Phaed.'

He hangs up.

A couple of older party-goers titter as they walk past her and her pile of mucus-coloured vomit. She can taste the vodka she had in the piña coladas earlier that night, this time more acidic, like dirty lake-water.

***

She makes it to the top of the High Street and turns left onto London Road. This is residential, a mix of red-brick and old, Edwardian houses, complete with the gables and porticoes. She feels like the worst of her journey is now over. She's almost there. Just down the road, up the hill to Edgar Mount, past the station, and boom, she's home as houses, her flatmate Denise probably waiting for her with a bowl of Cheerios and a cup of tea. That's their sisterly arrangement. When one is going out, the other stays up watching Netflix to make sure the other is safe. It started back when Denise was having the opposite problem to Phaedra. All her lovers seemed aggressive and needy and Denise would hate coming back to a dead house. So, they'd made a thing out of it, and it was pretty awesome and joyous.

Just thinking of it makes Phaedra feel safer.

But as she gets further along London Road, her heart sinks. There are police lights at the end of the road, yellow tape. The whole road has been closed off. As she approaches, a police constable steps forward.

'Sorry, you're going to have to take a step back, this is a crime scene.'

Phaedra can just see a small body, in the gap between two police cars; it's surrounded by men and women in full plastic anti-contamination suits. It looks like there has been an outbreak of some terrible virus.

Phaedra takes stock. There are other onlookers to the grisly spectacle. Other police officers are shooing them away. Blue and red lights deflect off the sightless windows of the residential homes here. It looks like the lights of one of the tacky bars back in the town.

She has a choice now: stay out all night, try and blitz through 'til morning, or take a trip around.

Then it hits her, if she doubles back, she can get to Old Bill's Station from the other side, cross over, then take the little gateway, which will lead her up a short little path between two rows of houses (basically through a few back gardens too) right past where the police have blocked off. It'll only add fifteen minutes to her journey, tops, and it's a lot shorter than going around Edgar Hill and coming at Maggy's Lane from the top.

'You out with a friend?' the cop asks.

Phaedra shakes her head.

'I'd recommend calling a taxi. I shouldn't say this, but it's a dangerous night to be out.'

The policeman is young, barely a speck of stubble on his chin. He's not yet been turned into a machine that will obey whatever inputs are inserted into it. He's looking at her, albeit probably his first thought is how attractive she is, but then there's a deep part of him that's just worried, one young person in a shit-screaming world to another. It's a ray of hope.

'I called ... the police ... earlier,' she stammers. 'About the park.' She lowers her voice to a whisper. 'Is there some kind of crazy man out there?'

The young man looks terrified. He swallows, looks behind him. Clearly his superior is knee-deep in post-mortem work. He turns back to Phaedra and silently nods.

'Get home safe. Taxi it.'

Phaedra nods. As she walks away, she hears a noise. It sounds every so faintly like a 'quack'. When she wheels around, the young police officer is staring at her, cross-browed, like *she's* the crazy one.

Hearing things. Seeing things.

Did you know, it's only the female mallards that make the traditional 'quack' sound.

She calls the taxi rank, even though her house is barely twenty minutes away. She's a walker, loves being outdoors. It was Miss Powell that first inspired in her that love. She used to take her students on nature walks. Miss Powell's Power Walks, the joke was.

She rings Fast Taxis first. After waiting five solid minutes on hold, she gets through.

'It'll be forty-five minutes, at least.' The administrator tells her. 'All our cars are out at the moment.'

Phaedra bounces from foot to foot. It's getting cold, the ice sinking into her joints like early-onset arthritis. She can't wait that long. She hangs up and calls another rank. The line's engaged. She grits her teeth.

The onlookers are clearing out now. The officer gives her a look that says she clearly cannot stay. Short-cut it is then, she doubles back, eventually finds the narrow side-alley that leads to Old Bill's.

A train passes through Old Bill's probably once every four-million years. It's leaf-strewn, rat-infested, with cracked tarmac, disintegrating under inconstant halogen lights. It's the kind of place where twelve-year-olds hang out and spray graffiti. There's almost always a resident tramp, wrapped up in sleeping bags and bin-liners.

Did you know that drakes will forcibly mate with any female that is isolated regardless of its species or whether they have a brood of ducklings already?

The causeway over the tracks is grimy, with plastic ripple-sheets tacked up over a metal girder latticework. It's hideous, but she doesn't need it to look pretty, she just needs it to get her to the other side.

As she sets foot on the opposite station, something catches her eye. It's a glint, the same glint that drew her eye across the lake. She *has* to turn towards it. It is movement her brain is hard-wired to *locate, locate, locate.*

Yes, the killer is standing in the middle of the tracks. He wears black office-trousers, black knee-high boots, and a black trench coat. The enfeebled lights shine on a rubbery mask shaped like a male duck's head, a fat bill poking out like a wad of papers. It is comical, ridiculous, made more ridiculous by the Halloween weapon in the killer's gloved hand. Phaedra isn't laughing. Her sphincter and throat tighten, reflexively, the way they do before an exam, only a thousand times worse. It is her body preparing for fight or flight, though neither seem good options.

The killer stares at her. She can see his eyes through sloppy holes cut in the mask. Bright, electric, wired. Coke-eyes.

Phaedra glances behind her. She can see the gate. It isn't locked. The killer isn't *that* far ahead of her.

Flight it is.

She breaks eye-contact first and runs. She doesn't want to give the killer any time, any time at all. She reaches the black gate, throws it open and takes the stairway two at a time as it snakes up to the same level as the residences. Gaining even ground, she pelts down the narrow avenue, gardens and unlit houses either side.

'Help, help, help!' she screams, at the top of her lungs. Lights flick on in one or two homes, but she has no idea what good it will do, whether anyone will come out. She remembers that you are supposed to scream 'fire' when being attacked by a rapist, because people are more likely to come running, but that seems to be just a confusion of matters, and besides, her brain is devoting 90% of its processing power to *left foot, right foot*. Amazing, how someone like her, on her way to a Masters in Biology, requires so much RAM for such a simple physical act.

Twisting, left, then right, like running through a maze. Shit, she realises she's lost. In her efforts to lose him, she's made a wrong turn. *Fuck, fuck, fuck, fuck.*

She dares to stop for a moment.

Instantly, she is caught, a black gloved hand clapping on her forearm. The grip is barbaric, needling. She turns and throws a punch with all her might. It slaps against the mask. She expects the mask to fold, crumple, for there to be nothing underneath, but her fist meets something hard, a skull. A yelp escapes the killer's lips. The grip slackens. She twists from it and runs.

Not quick enough. She feels a hard boot in her back, topples forward. She crashes through a fence; it snaps easy as cardboard, and she is suddenly tumbling down a hill, towards the tracks.

Head over heels, limbs cracking, dress tearing. She slams into a barbed wire fence. Her back is torn up. She feels like someone has put her in a blender.

The killer stands at the top of the hill, looking down on her. It reminds her then of the drakes, circling and circling and circling, just waiting for the female to run out of breath, tucker out. Well, she'll not fucking tucker out, she'll keep fucking running forever if she has to.

She crawls, frantic, a mouse exposed to flame. Like some kind of magic, she finds exactly what she is looking for, a way out of this barbed trap. There's a maintenance hatch, presumably for the electrics. Normally, they can't be opened unless you have the right tools, but this one has already been popped. A stroke of luck.

She lifts the rusted lid, slides her feet in first, down the ladder into the dark.

***

Her iPhone serves as a torch, a sepulchral blue light filling up a cylindrical tunnel. This place is bigger than she expected, more like a sewer than an electrical maintenance room. Maybe she was wrong.

She jogs down the tunnel, aware of how the floor is carpeted with a two-inch thick layer of faeces and scum and she is walking in it bare foot. No time to worry now. A bath can fix that. A bath can't fix her being raped and killed. Or, somehow worse, killed, then raped. She suspects it is the latter, from what she saw at the lake. That is what truly disturbs her.

The tunnel goes on for what feels like hours, a dark straight line to nowhere. She is waiting for another maintenance hatch. It's not a big city, wherever she ends up she will be able to call a taxi or even walk.

But no hatch so far. The tunnel slopes downward. She hesitates, remembers what happened the last time she paused, takes a deep breath of corrupted air and heads on.

There is a light at the bottom of the tunnel. Firelight, flames in an old oil-drum, like something from a post-apocalyptic vision, or scenes from downtown Detroit.

There is a *thing* standing next to the oil drum. Vaguely human,

19

but hunched over, bent double. As she draws closer, its face catches the light and she realises it is a duck with human features, or perhaps a human with duck features. No mask. Its bulbous belly is propped up on two bright orange stalks of legs. Its bill glistens, greenish bile at the edges. Its eyes are dull.

She has never seen anything so awful in her whole life.

It waddles around, searching for little tidbits—god knows what— in the layers of shit. The duck person is fucking five feet tall. It has a vaguely human chest, the remnants of a spinal column, jutting vertebrae cresting its back. The rest is all feathers.

Phaedra is sure she's having a break with reality.

The tunnel levels. She sees more duck people, more trash fires. Some of the duck people are rutting on grimy rugs, their awkward bodies gyrating like badly put-together gears. She sees the glimpse of the duck corkscrew penis, only this one is human-sized and about as thick as a Pringles can, writhing around like a snake, trying to find the right vagina hole.

Did you know: Female mallards have phantom vaginas so only the most dexterous, or freakish, males can impregnate them.

Ducks are absolutely fucked.

Donald Duck terrifies her. Daffy Duck terrifies her. They're all slobbering, angry rapists. The actual term for duck breeding behaviour is 'Attempted Rape Flight'.

She collapses against a grimy wall, closes her eyes. She needs to get through this, she needs to *get out of this nightmare.* Her Master's degree brain is telling her that none of this can be real. Ducks cannot grow to five feet tall, just as they cannot have semi-human traits, like fucked up spines or vaguely human teeth inside their bills. No. These things are not scientific.

No part of her wants to remember or study these creatures.

The tunnel widens into a chamber. Black sewage flows from a rusted pipe, filling up a turgid, indeterminably deep, square pool. Ducks glide over the dark waters, these ones also human-sized. One male spots her, boils blossoming out of the side of its ugly face, a kind of golden chain around its fat neck. It quacks angrily, grinding its human teeth together, making a noise like rock crumbling.

She runs, around the edges of the lake. It is all monstrous.

But there is the ladder and the hatch. She could cry, cry at the sight of a mildewed, mouldy ladder. She climbs up, fingers numb and joints clicking; exits into . . .

***

An actual labyrinth, with fifty-foot-high stone walls emitting no light. She stands on a slightly raised platform. Below her, the water is waist deep. Normal-sized ducks drift everywhere, ghosts on the river of the dead.

The hatch is still there beneath her, but she has no desire to go back down. She cannot. Will not.

She is not in the city anymore. That much is clear. Nothing tonight has been what it seems. She is more scared than she has ever been in her life. Most of all, she is scared of seeing herself. She is battered, bruised, muddy, crazy—she will not recognise the woman she sees in the mirror when she gets home. *If* she gets home. It is a big if. Rules are bending. Denise and Netflix and Cheerios feel like fantasies.

She lowers herself into the bleak waters and walks.

The sewer-maze is looping, a mindfuck. Stairways, doors, but never any true features. The tiled, grungy walls are markless and she cannot mark them, not even with her nails. Everything seems to circle back around to the same corridors, though she can never find the hatch again. She is so tired, her feet ache. She knows if she stops moving, stops *flying,* the drake will catch her, drown her, just like the one she saw at the start of this dreadful ordeal.

I must keep moving. She thinks of Miss Powell, those power walks, how she would hum a little ditty, a little marching tune.

'Come on, students,' she'd say, all perky and sassy and sexy. *God, I want to be like her,* Phaedra had thought, *so confident and so attractive and so clever*. All the boys drooled over her.

She hears the tune now, the one Miss Powell used to hum. It is her guiding beacon as she struggles at sea, the noise of home calling. She forces one foot in front of the other even though her feet are practically worn down to nubs.

Finally, she stumbles. The tune is not leading her anywhere, just round and round.

No, she must go on.

There's a light at the end of the tunnel, literally.

She grips the wall for support, uses it to steady herself, keeps walking.

MALLARD'S MAZE

There's an altar, at the end of the tunnel: a place where the tunnel becomes a circular chamber. Somehow, she has found the centre of this corkscrew maze. There is a skeleton, that of a tremendous mallard, the size of an elephant, perhaps larger; it is surrounded by dripping wax candles. Lesser mallards quack and waddle at its feet.

Eyeless sockets bore into her, eternally thirsting.

Every aspect of the monolithic skeleton is phallic: its ribs, its colossal bill—like a slab of marble cut from an ancient temple. The longer she looks at it, the more she feels like she has left the world she knew behind. Strange thoughts whirl through her head. She sees carnal gods with donkey and rabbit and deer faces, dancing around the bonfires of the Mallard King, orgying in the thrashing nest of its manhood. All of those gods, the oldest and the darkest and strongest, all of them nothing, all of them bowed before this mighty unconquerable effigy. Its kingdom is eternal, before time; it is the violent genesis of all things. When it divided water from water, making sky and sea, it was only to rape that which lay between.

The killer is there, kneeling, staring at her, mask lit by the candles. Breath catches in Phaedra's throat.

'Ducks are the most perfect sexual specimens,' a familiar voice says.

The killer removes the mask.

It is Denise.

For a moment, Phaedra cannot speak. Denise has one of those kind, soft faces that could completely disarm even the hardest nutter in the jailhouse: with rosy cheeks, and a big teeth-filled smile that actually sparkles. She has frizzy hair, wears little makeup because her skin does that work for her. She describes herself as a chocolate angel.

Now, she is grinning at Phaedra.

'Denny? Den—' Phaedra tastes stomach-acid at the back of her throat.

'Yeah. Surprise, right?'

Phaedra tries to hold herself upright by clinging to the wall, but she fails and slumps down. Denise crouches over her.

'You know, I just got so tired of you dating every fucker who walked in off the street except me. Like, "hello", Phaedra. I'm right fucking here.' Denise slaps her chest, grins impishly, flicks her hair from her eyes. Phaedra can make out individual droplets of sweat on her face. 'You weren't getting the messages. You know, Netflix and chill means *fucking*, right? It's a euphemism. Didn't they teach you that on your Master's?' Denise makes quotation mark signs with her fingers. 'So, I thought I'd try a bit of an aggressive strategy.'

'But . . . but you . . . killed people?' Phaedra cannot begin to understand the words leaving her lips.

'Yeah, babe. I did. Killed one on London Road to block your egress. Killed one in the park to get you going.'

More troubling to Phaedra than that, though, bizarre and awful though she knows it is, is how Denise knew what Miss Powell—good, wonderful, inspiring Miss Powell—had said to her all those years ago. How she knew just how fucking shit-scared of ducks Phaedra has been her whole life, ever since Miss Powell's lessons. It's partly her fear that has compelled her down the biology path, a kind of fascinated disgust.

Denise seems to read this question off her eyes.

'Babe, you talk about that teacher non-fucking-stop. "She was a dream, Denise". "She was fucking god on earth, Denise". You must have quoted her twenty fucking times, sister.' Denise chuckles. Laughing is the last thing Phaedra can do right now. 'You talk in your sleep too. And sing.'

'But . . . this?'

'Oh, the maze? Yeah. A little special something from me too.'

'Oh God, oh God my head hurts.'

'Yeah, it does the first time, hun. It'll get easier.'

'Oh *Gooooddddd*.'

'Whoa, sis. Never knew you were religious. Ain't that a conflict of interests with your whole science vibe?'

'Are you gonna kill me?' Phaedra whispers.

Denise looks at her. Phaedra has a strange thought as she returns Denise's gaze. *You're a man in there,* she thinks. *A drake. And this, all of this, is your version of the corkscrew dick. Only, instead of the dick bending and twisting, it's reality you're fucking with. It's a corkscrew in your head.*

'You gotta give me what I need, Phaed.'

Denise unzips her trousers, pulls them down. Uncurling from

where her human genitals should be is a dark, twisting phallus. It spirals towards her, hypnotic, like it is smelling its way towards her.

Phaedra trembles. She is sickened, feels like she wants to just vomit herself to death, but she knows now she must be stronger than ever.

Somewhere, she can hear Miss Powell, her happy tune. If only she knew where Phaedra was now, how fucked it all was, victim of her darling little creatures. Phaedra blames her, absolutely and wholeheartedly. It is all she has left.

The corkscrew thing has almost snaked around her. Denise is biting her lower lip, eyes burning, hungrier even than the dead eyes of the god-mallard.

'Come on, just taste it. I want it in your mouth first,' Denise says.

Phaedra takes a deep breath.

Here, in this corkscrew reality, she has only one hope. She must become Phaed. She must become the ghost that everyone always thought she was.

Did you know: female mallards have phantom vaginas?

She must accept to survive.

She takes it, down her throat. She has never liked this aggressive act of dominance; never had a partner who reciprocated particularly well either, even Jen.

Denise forces it down her throat, or perhaps it wriggles of its own accord, into the oesophagus. She gags. The taste is disgusting, like rotten meat. She is going to be sick again. Her gorge is rising, tightening.

'Just a little deeper, baby,' Denise says, closing her eyes.

Deep enough, Phaedra thinks.

She bites.

Denise screams and screams.

Phaedra throws up, spitting out a mouthful of blood and a wiry hunk of flesh. She grimaces, wipes the blood from her lips with the back of her hand.

'I'll kill you, bitch! I'll kill you!' Denise screams. The knife is in her hand.

Phaedra charges her, howling, a good old fashioned shoulder-barge. It takes Denise by surprise. She expected fear and defence. She stumbles back from the impact, slips on her mallard-mask, and impales herself on one of the almighty mallard ribs. It juts from her chest, a pallid little parasite emerged to light.

The thing between Denise's legs twitches, spasms, leaking like a shower-head. The little ducks happily splash through the blood, washing their feathers with it.

'Fuck . . . ' Denise chokes. *'Fucking bitch.'*

'Yeah. *I'm* the bitch.' She spits out blood and scum. 'Go fuck yourself, Denise.'

Denise grins like a user who's found their first high in a long time. She even laughs, a soft *wahwahwah* which sounds like a duck's quack. Or maybe Phaedra's head is just fucked.

There's a ladder, beside the altar. Phaedra wasn't sure if it was there before, but she doesn't care. She just wants to be out of this place, to never see a fucking duck again in her life.

She begins to climb.

Denise calls out to her.

'Phaedra . . . Phaedra!'

She pauses, looks down at Denise. She's already turning white as the bones behind her, blood drained out.

'This never would have happened if you'd just accepted me. If you'd just fucking paid me a bit of attention.'

Phaedra rolls her eyes.

'Sure, this is *my* fault.'

She reaches the top of the ladder.

'Fuck you Phaedra!' Hatred in every line. Her lips are pouted, duck-like, petulant. 'Fuck you!'

'No, Denise. You never will.'

She opens the hatch and regains the cool peaceful air in wonder.

***

As she sees the familiar street-sign for Maggy's Lane, Phaedra takes a moment. The cops are still looking for the killer, but she doubts they will ever find her. Phaedra is not even sure it is a place that she has been to, more a part of her own head. But Denise was there. Or maybe she wasn't? Maybe Phaedra will open the door and find the real Denise smiling back at her. She hopes not. She's not sure she could ever look at her the same again.

As she reaches the front door, she sees there is a speckled female mallard, tucked away on her front porch. It looks like it is nursing an injured leg. Its brown eyes peer up at her, half expecting attack.

'It's okay. I won't hurt you,' Phaedra says. 'You're better off here than that lake.'

Seemingly smiling, the duck nestles back down into its feathers and sleeps.

Did you know: ducks are an invasive species?

Phaedra carefully steps over the mallard, unlocks the door. No Denise waiting for her, the house is empty. Good. She strips off. Takes a hot shower. As the blood washes off from her, corkscrewing into the plughole, she cries. Not because she's scared, or because of the horrible thing she had to do.

She cries because she thinks: *I'm so glad to be human.*

Salivation

THEODORE DEADRAT

I **MUST HAVE SEEN** him hundreds of times, never looking twice, before the morning he caught my eye. I don't tend to notice specific faces. I work in data entry, which means most of my day passes in a gray haze of screens flickering like ghosts and keys clicking like bones, counting the number of keystrokes left between me and my grave. I don't look up. I don't notice the gray sky anymore, or the gray subway train as it rattles up to the platform, squealing as if in pain. I don't look at the faces packed all around me on the platform, the train, or on the street. Just animals going about their business—goats, such as myself, and other ungulates, rodents, and the occasional predator—eyes invariably downcast.

That day, however, was a little different. I was agitated. Angry. I don't remember why—it could have been as simple as an ugly dream the night before. I spat on the ground more than once as I stomped through the rain to the subway and stabbed the slot with my token as if avenging a wrong. I stood simmering on the platform, hating the faceless shapes of the animals. I imagined they could sense it. I imagined they were afraid.

That was the first time I saw him—I mean, *really* saw him. He was a deer, cinnamon brown, pushing the gray of the rest of the world out of its way, antlers filed down to nubs—an affectation of youth or femininity, often employed by males of antlered species to communicate a romantic leaning toward other stags. That brazenness, and, of course, his lithe figure, almost immediately set my imagination to work concocting daydreams not at all conducive to a peaceful train ride. Mercifully, when at last we both disembarked, he turned one way while I turned another. It did not seem as though he had noticed me at all.

After that, I noticed him every morning. It was maddening. Each day's commute was spent trying not to sneak glances and failing repeatedly; trying to stem a flow of impure thoughts and failing repeatedly; promising each day to pay him no mind the next—and failing repeatedly. I only ever saw him in the morning, for a few minutes each day, though as weeks passed, and my obsession grew, I found him occupying my thoughts. The daydreams, at first limited to our shared subway ride, began to intrude upon my concentration at work, and my increasingly fitful sleep at home. I realized I was going mad. I realized I was in love.

Of course, the more reasonable part of me knew it was a fantasy with no grounding in reality. This stag was nearly a decade my junior, and of course we were different species—not unheard-of, but certainly a stumbling block in a budding relationship, as an infinitude of songs and poetry could attest. Still, the harder I fought to banish him from my thoughts, the more persistently he featured in my imagination. My work, already a haze of dull discomfort, faded even further into the background of my daily existence. I barely slept. I barely ate. I existed only when riding the train; only for a few minutes each morning; only when I could be near him.

This had been the state of things for a few months when I realized I had to eat him.

To be clear, to kill and eat another person, regardless of species, was not a thing that had ever crossed my mind before. Predators and prey have lived in relative harmony for centuries, and common wisdom held that we had evolved beyond one species feeding on another. Certainly, prejudices still exist, cultural and psychological differences between species that can never be fully bridged even by the ever-onward march of civilization. Belonging to a prey species myself, I knew I might never fully understand the experience of being a predator. That said, animals of all species had lived and worked together in society for a very long time. Murder in any form, especially predation, was a criminal act—one it had never even crossed my mind to commit. That is, of course, until it did.

I still rode the train, of course. I still eagerly anticipated seeing that beautiful deer every morning. At first, I ignored how I began to salivate when I looked at him. I ignored how bloody my daydreams, which before had been merely lewd, had become. I tried not to attribute too much significance how my lunches—salads of greens and root vegetables—began to seem less appetizing each day. I tried not to attribute too much significance to my dreams, even when I awoke suddenly at night, sweaty, painfully aroused—and hungry.

Eventually, I decided that the thing to do was to stop riding the train. I bought a bicycle, and resolved to pedal myself to work each day, putting thoughts of the deer out of my mind. It was folly, of course. My attempt served only to highlight my weakness, or perhaps how far I had gone down the path to insanity. I would set out for work with time to spare, only to find myself lingering by the entrance to the subway, watching for him. I remember feeling my heart jump when I saw him emerge from the crowd of morning pedestrians, and I had to force myself not to follow him. This happened multiple days in a row, causing me to be late to work, which in turn nearly cost me my job. It troubled me, even more than the dreams had, to discover that I couldn't bear to miss out on seeing the object of my obsession. If this was love, then I had never really been in love before. I had never experienced an attraction so intense.

And, of course, I still dreamed every night about eating him.

The day finally came that I worked up the nerve to approach him. I called in sick that day, but went down to the subway as usual, and disembarked when he did. I touched his arm to get his attention and he smiled at me—sadly, it seemed, in retrospect. His eyes were vast, labyrinthine, and he was so quiet and accommodating in every way. Of course he had noticed my attention. Of course he would join me for coffee, maybe breakfast. Of course he would love to see my apartment. Of course we could take my car. It was almost too easy; followed the plot of my dreams almost exactly; made what was to come seem utterly inevitable. His gentle smile and subtle aura of sadness suggested that he knew from the start what I was going to do, what I *had* to do.

We made love first. It would have been gauche not to. Tender, but joyless: perfunctory. Final. In that moment, I knew we loved one another, and I also knew that he had foreseen and resigned himself to his fate. I don't think I was even capable of hiding the look of hunger in my eyes anymore. When I slit his throat, he put his hand on my wrist and looked up into my eyes as if to say: "Of course."

I had never eaten, or even prepared, meat before. I didn't know what I was doing; I cut clumsily, ate awkwardly, cried incessantly. The meal I made of my beloved deer felt simultaneously like an utter sacrilege and the perfect ending to a fairytale. A lot of fairytales end that way, after all, with someone being eaten. That night, I didn't dream at all, and from that day on, I never felt love or sexual desire again. It was as if I had swallowed my hopes and dreams along with the meat.

Days passed. Weeks. I cleaned the apartment feverishly, purchasing supplies in small amounts at different shops around the city, until I was satisfied that no trace of my deed remained for a casual visitor to discover. I went back to work right away, a new sort of calm having come over me, resigned to the gray, quiet life that had been only briefly interrupted by intense obsession. I still rode the subway every day, gaze fixed on a hole in the crowd shaped like the deer I had met in that strange dream. Until one morning I caught another's gaze fixated upon me.

It was a mouse, barely visible in the crowd, so small and quiet, all white and pink and fidgeting nervously. I had never noticed him on the subway before, which was hardly surprising, but that day something about him caught my eye. I noticed that he was staring at me intently, a blush reddening his little ears. Little pink paws firmly grasping the pole for support. Mouth slightly agape.

A thin trickle of saliva glistened on his chin.

THE HAMFORD PIGS

N. ROSE

IN THE LATE '80S, my dad founded the Tremorn Farm Pigs, a club made up from selected members of the Hamford police station. Nothing official, of course. There wasn't a rulebook or a secret handshake; they didn't go out for drinks on a Friday night, or hold fundraisers, or any of that crap. What they did have, courtesy of a dead uncle my dad couldn't stand, was twenty acres of land away from prying eyes (the aforementioned Tremorn Farm), complete with a big old barn that was mostly still standing, a handful of rusting farm machines, and an endless supply of dead pigs.

Dad died in '99, when I was eighteen and trying to decide between dropping straight into a dead-end job or spending a few years at university first. I always imagined it would be one of the bad guys that got the old bastard. Maybe a tyre iron to the back of the head, something like that. Something proper for a man's man like him. Turned out I couldn't have been more wrong. Hours away from ringing in the new millennium, there he is with his latest boyfriend's dick up his arsehole and his heart just up and explodes like a fucking party popper. No warning shot across the bow, no doctor telling him to cut back on the alcohol and the fags. Just wham, bam, thank you and goodnight.

Anyway, a thing like that, it changes a person.

So I flipped university the bird and joined the police, following in the old man's footsteps. In my head it was going to be all beat-downs and busts, like some sort of American cop show. Yeah, maybe over there things are like that. Here in the English West Country a new bobby gets the shit nobody else wants. The community service

31

calls, the disputes between neighbours, the piss-heads throwing up on your shoes on a Friday night. And every other night, for that matter. But that's not to say that the tip of England's cock is completely without its hardened criminals. Fuck, if that was the case the Pigs would never have been needed in the first place.

And they were needed. Not often, but not that rare either, if you know what I mean.

With me being Pig royalty, so to speak, it was only a year and a few months after I joined the force before the current club president pulled me aside for a few choice words. Vickers Bissoe, a guy who looked like he could rip apart a bear with his hands and teeth, had been like a scary uncle to me growing up, but I could tell by the look on his face that this was business.

"Toby," he said, as he pulled me to one side. "You know about the Pigs then, boy?"

"Not really, Vick," I told him, and meant it. Dad never said much, and by that I mean he told me fuck-all.

"We're doing one tonight. I can get you in. You want in?"

I shrugged. I mean, it wasn't something I'd really thought about. "Not really, Vick," I said again, and that made him laugh.

"I'll get you in. The farm, seven. If you're late, you're fucked."

I watched him as he walked away, thinking about what my mum would say. Men being men. That was what she used to tell me when I was a kid, if I ever asked why I couldn't go up to the farm with my dad. But that was before dad started sucking dick behind her back, and the divorce and everything, and after that her opinion was less men being men and more men *doing* men. So, I couldn't help wondering if that 'you're fucked' comment was meant literally. But try as I might to imagine Vick and the boys having a big gay orgy up at the old barn I just couldn't picture it, and—screw it—I was curious anyway, so I decided it was time to see what went on up at Tremorn Farm.

At that time, me and Morwenna Yeo—who I would later marry and swear to honour in sickness and health and all that—were living in sin. I already knew she was special though—a real nice girl. Sweet. A bit on the large side, but I never did understand what men see in skin and bones. A girl like Morwenna makes everything a little more comfortable, if you know what I mean. And the fact she came with a kid in tow didn't bother me one bit. I liked kids, I guess, in a lot of ways, I still was one myself.

I called her to let her know that I wouldn't be home until late. Told her, "Warm the bed for me, yeah? And leave the door unlocked."

She laughed. "You have a high opinion of yourself, Toby Rogers. Maybe I'll just finger myself and go to sleep. You can sleep in your car."

I laughed, knowing she would leave the door unlocked like I asked. "Say hi to Edward for me, tell him I'll see him in the morning before school."

"I will. See you later, darlin'. Have fun on your bust or whatever."

"I will."

I hung up the phone without telling her I wasn't going on a bust or whatever. It wouldn't do her any harm to think that her man was out catching criminals instead of swigging beer and watching porn, or whatever the guys did out at the pig farm.

***

Just before seven, I pulled up outside the barn at Tremorn Farm, parking my beat up old Vauxhall beside half a dozen other cars. Vick was a detective, and I was guessing the other guys probably were as well. Jaguars and Mercedes Benzes don't get bought on a recruit's salary, that's for sure.

The place didn't belong to my family anymore. When dad died, he left me his car and left my mum a little bit of cash he had saved. The farm went to Vick, in trust for the club, and that suited me and mum just fine. I mean, what the fuck would we want with a pig farm anyway? So we let that slide quite happily, and I sold the car to buy myself a nice TV and speaker system: proper dog's bollocks setup with a subwoofer that could make a man shit himself at twenty paces.

"Fuck, Vick, I can smell you from here," I said as he walked across the yard towards me.

He grinned. "Proper country smell, boy. Besides, you get used to it. First time at the farm, is it?"

"I came here once when dad inherited the place. Didn't think much of it; thought it smelled of pig shit. Which makes me wonder, who looks after the pigs nowadays?"

"Old boy came with the place, keeps the pigs. Keeps out of our way, too. Knows not to go in the barn, and that's all as matters. Any profits beyond the upkeep, he gets to take home."

"Sounds like he gets a good deal."

"We all get a good deal. You coming inside or just standing out here all night?"

"What goes on inside?"

"Not out here," he said, glancing around like someone might be listening in. Then he beckoned, and I followed.

Inside the front door of the barn there was a kind of makeshift lobby area. It clearly hadn't been part of the original structure, what with chipboard used for floor and walls and ceiling, like we were standing inside a wooden box, all left unpainted and uncovered. The room was maybe ten feet long by six wide, and it had a table with chairs, a kettle and sink, and two wooden chests that looked like they came off a pirate ship. Apart from that it was empty, just a door leading outside and another directly opposite.

"Nobody else here?" I asked, glancing around.

"Everyone's inside, Toby. Just you and me right here, and it's time to get serious. In a minute you're going to see something, and it's a thing that you might not like much at first. But you've gotta give me your word that you'll not tell nobody else. I mean it, boy: nobody." I was about to protest, tell him I didn't know if I could promise something like that, seeing as he just told me I might not like it, but he held up a hand to silence me. "Two things you should know. First, all this was your old man's idea. Now, that should tell you something about the morality of it, because we both know your dad was a churchgoing man."

I nodded. Vick had a point. Apart from the adultery, I'd never known my dad to do anything that wasn't right and proper. Hell, once I'd seen him drive back ten miles to a petrol station when we were out in the countryside with my mum, because he realised they gave him too much change when he filled up. Hell, even with the fucking around behind mum's back, he didn't try to make excuses once he was caught. Full confession time, it was. I knew he didn't always stick within the law when he was catching the bad guys, but he always stuck within God's laws every day of his adult life. Even my mum would have grudgingly admitted that.

"And the second thing?"

"Second thing is the same as me and your father told each of the guys in there." He pointed his thumb over his shoulder at the inner door. "You see what's going on here, you give me a chance to explain why it is the way it is. You don't like it, well, there's not a lot any of us can do about that. You turn around and you walk back out. But you tell another soul what you saw and I let all of those guys off the leash. You're on your own. You understand?"

"What if I can't promise that?"

He shrugged. "Then you leave right now."

I thought about that for a moment. I mean, I'd known Vick as long as I could remember, and although he and my mum didn't always see eye to eye, especially as Vick had known about my dad's other life long before she found out, she'd always trusted him. Said I could go to him just as I could go to my father. And whatever was going on in there, in a way it was my birthright to see it. I mean, my dad would have wanted me to be here, to follow in his footsteps. Right?

"All right, Vick, I'll take a look."

"Good boy." He looked me up and down. "Now strip."

"Pardon me?"

"You don't go in there while there's any chance you're wearing a wire. Besides, clothes pick up DNA like a dog picks up fleas. What's going on in the barn ain't exactly legal, and anything you're wearing might be the thing that gets us all caught. We all strip. We got a bunch of showers rigged up inside and we all shower off when we're done. Then we get dressed and we're good to go." He pulled his grey T-shirt up over his head, then opened one of the chests. "You can put your clothes in here."

***

Vick stripped out of his clothes like there was nothing to it, and I guess he'd been doing this long enough that it wasn't really an issue for him. Vest, trousers, boxer shorts, shoes and socks—all of them went in the chest so that he was standing there with his dick hanging loose and his body hair on full display.

For me, this was all new. A moment passed where I seriously reconsidered my decision to go through with it. But with Vick's eyes on me, I couldn't quite bring myself to say the words and leave it all behind. So, reluctantly, I started taking my own clothes off until I was buck naked and covering my embarrassment with cupped hands.

"You got a boner or something?" Vick stared at my crotch.

"No."

"Then let it hang free, boy. There's nobody here that's going to judge you for what you got down there."

When I didn't take my hands away, he shook his head in frustration, leaned down and flipped open the second chest. Then he reached inside and in a single motion lobbed something rubbery my way.

Of course, my reactions were quick and automatic. I grabbed the missile out of the air without even thinking about the fact I was leaving myself uncovered. By the time I realised, I was already on full display.

"That was a dirty trick."

Vick grinned. "Had to be done. You know they can make cameras small enough these days you could have had one hiding under there, right?"

"Fuck off," I said. "What is this thing, anyway?"

I turned the object over in my hands, not much liking the way it felt against my skin. Kind of leathery, with little hairs sticking out here and there.

"Pigskin," Vick said.

"Say again?"

I don't know if he repeated it, because when I realised what I was holding I screamed like an arachnophobe in a spider house, dropped the thing on the floor, and took an instinctive step back.

"The *fuck*?"

Vick was laughing. "It's a pigskin. We're the Tremorn Farm Pigs, boy. That right there was your dad's, the first pigskin we ever cut. Been used a few times, too, I can tell you. But he looked after it and I expect you to do the same. Treat it with leather conditioner when we're done—you'll find some in the chest—wipe off any spills; put it away carefully."

"What's it for?" I stared at the pigskin, lying there on the floor, not sure if I even wanted to touch it again. It's not that I'm squeamish, but I mean . . . Jesus, he might have warned me.

Vick didn't say a word. He grabbed another from the chest, opened it out like it was a mask, then put it on top of his head without pulling it over his face, so that the snout was sticking out in the middle of his forehead like some sort of horn.

"You're not seriously expecting me to wear that thing?"

He shook his head. "It's hard to explain until you put it on and head through that door, but there's more to the pigskin than just a way to hide your face. You get that on, you channel the spirit of the pig it once belonged to. I know, I know, sounds crazy, but it's true. We all felt it. Hell, your dad was the first to notice. That spirit starts to guide you, like it's fused with your own brain, and it's angry, Toby. Fuck, is it angry. That pig remembers everything that was done to it and it wants to make someone else suffer the way it suffered at the end, maybe worse."

"Sounds crazy all right. What, I'm going to be snuffling around on all fours looking for pigswill?"

"No. You'll still be you, but you won't be a hundred percent you. Every part of you will also be partly the pig." He took a deep breath. "Look, just put the fucking thing on your head and you'll see what I mean. You ready?"

***

How he persuaded me to do it, I still have no idea. I mean, that pigskin was foul. I swear it still stank like pork. But in the end, I picked it up from the floor, took a deep breath and pulled it over my head.

And fuck if he wasn't right.

The second it was on, I felt a kind of change, like I was seeing through new eyes. And I was hungry. Desperate for something, though at that moment I couldn't have said what. But, given that my dad had been dead for a couple of years, I guess that pigskin hadn't seen any action for long enough that it was itching to stretch its legs.

"One last thing," Vick said, his voice a little more gruff under the mask, like he was snuffling or grunting along with his words. "In there, you don't speak. Not a word. We've got a video camera set up and recording, and we don't want no voices coming through on the tape. Got it?"

"Not a word," I repeated.

"Good boy. You go through, you take a look, and we come back here for a discussion."

THE HAMFORD PIGS

He didn't wait another moment. He walked over to the door, rapped sharply, and, after a few seconds, there was a click and a loud *thunk* as a lock and a deadbolt were thrown back. The door opened and I followed Vick into the barn.

It was an enormous space: probably thirty feet in either direction and mostly empty. Bare bulbs had been strung up at irregular intervals from the high rafters, lighting up the floor beneath them, then fading to shadows quickly. The corners were still in shade, as was the roof high above, but I could see sharp blades and farm tools around the edges of the barn: forks and scythes and rakes that had probably last seen active duty in the reign of the first Queen Elizabeth.

And, in the middle of the barn, there was a thin, lanky feller stripped to his underwear and hung—by his bare ankles—from one of the beams. His head didn't quite touch the floor, but his hands hung down so they could scramble at the dry dirt. And scramble they did, desperately trying to exert some control over the situation he was in. What I remember the most was the noises he was making. Someone had pulled an old sack over his head, and tied it at his throat, and I was guessing that underneath he had some sort of gag, since he wasn't pleading or shouting obscenities. No—Jesus—this was something else. Half a dozen men, naked except for the pigskins they wore, stood around him with broken wooden poles they were using as makeshift clubs. Without a word, each lined up a shot and let rip, beating him about the stomach and chest so that he swung back-and-forth and around and around. And with each dull thud of a club, the guy let out the most pitiful cry. Not shrill, not sickening, just exhausted and pained. His flesh where they beat him was dark and pulpy, swollen and soft, and the rope around his legs was stained dark red with drawn blood.

What surprised me most was how my mind reacted to what I was seeing. In the cold light of day, later, I would almost throw up when I thought about that scene. But, in that moment, my heart leaped at the sight, adrenalin pumping, like I was in for a treat.

I glanced back at Vick, and he nodded, ushering me back through the door and closing it behind him. He pulled the pigskin up off his face, like maybe he couldn't talk while under its influence, and I did the same.

"Toby, boy, that feller in there's our guest speaker for tonight's Pig gathering. Andy Nancarrow. Or as CID like to call him, The Hamford Kiddie Fiddler."

"Say again?"

"Well, last time this fucker had any dealings with us was before your time. Brought in for jerking off to photos of little girls and boys. Right dirty bastard. But you heard about the bodies recently, right?"

"Five-year-old girls?"

"Both strangled; both molested before they died." Vick shook his head and made a noise in the back of his throat, like he might throw up at the thought of it. "Poor little things. I knew the mother of one. You know how that affects a family? Jesus, I can't even imagine what she's going through, knowing that happened to her little girl."

I felt another surge of adrenalin. My limbs were moving on their own, and I knew what direction they wanted to go. I wanted to be in there. I wanted to break that fucker's legs with the blunt end of an axe.

"And he's the one's responsible?"

Vick nodded. "Obviously progressed from the photos. Should have put him down, if you ask me, not given him a couple years suspended."

"Motherfucker."

"These judges aren't in touch with reality, if you ask me. But the thing is, as much evidence as we have, it's still not enough to get him off the streets. Means waiting around until he makes a mistake."

I shook my head. "So what? We beat a confession out of him? Count me in."

"Wouldn't do any good. I mean, sure, he'll confess. They always do. But this isn't an interview, and nor is it a courtroom. Nancarrow's guilty—end of story. Judge and jury have already spoken, and that just leaves the executioner."

That took me aback. I mean, beating a guy is one thing. Getting a confession, sure. But . . . "We're going to kill him?"

Vick nodded. "But first, he has to be made to suffer. See, the video tape goes away to a sympathetic lawyer to keep until the last of us passes away. Then those tapes, they go to the media. Nobody knows whether the Pigs are still in business, and maybe those bad guys that are still around think about confessing what they've done rather than be strung up like the others in the tapes. You get what I mean?"

I nodded, wordless. What he was saying made sense. As I was mulling it over, it struck me that, a moment before, when I had the pigskin over my head, I wouldn't have needed any time to consider. Hell, if he'd put one of those wooden sticks in my hand when we were in the barn I would have set about sticking Andy Nancarrow with the pointed end, and that without knowing what he'd done.

"He sure deserves it," I said.

"That he does, that he does. So, you're okay with this?"

Before I answered, I pulled the pigskin down over my face. As the tanned flesh covered my eyes, as the snout fell into place over my nose, as my mouth lined up with that of the pig that once owned it, I felt myself grow porkier, more bacon-like, and I felt the hunger rise inside me. And I knew what that hunger was, too. It was for blood.

I nodded, turned and rapped on the door. And that was when the real fun began.

***

Something inside me knew how to be a pig in that barn. As I stepped through the door and saw Nancarrow strung there, looking like a punch bag, I started to crouch low, to grunt and oink, and the others replied in the same way.

But nobody handed me a stick. It seems like that was just the pre-game warm up, because as soon as Vick stepped inside the barn everyone kind of hung back and stopped what they were doing, letting him advance until he was face to face with the dirty little fucker. Or face to knees, I should say, since Vick was on his feet and Nancarrow was strung up by his ankles.

And, if that bastard thought the beating was the worst he was going to face, he was wrong. Vick crouched low, close to his face, and started snuffling like he was trying to work out if Nancarrow might make a good meal, and Nancarrow's head twitched back and forth, up and down, using any strength he had left to try to locate the source of the new noises. And as I watched, a wet patch appeared on the front of his underwear, grew darker and larger. Urine trickled down the sicko's stomach, running over his chest, his neck and in a single dark stream beneath the sack blindfold.

The smell was acrid and sharp, like he'd been holding it for a while.

I have no idea how long he'd been hanging there. Could have been all day. But despite everything he must have endured, it wasn't until Vick got up close and personal like that that he pissed himself. I had to hand it to the guy—I know I wouldn't have held out that long.

Vick started grunting and oinking even louder then, and the other guys joined in too. And to my surprise, I found myself making the same noises like we were some sort of pig clan. The cacophony was so loud, I barely registered that Andy Nancarrow was also making noises. But his were the panicked, bleating noises of an animal that knows it's caught, that knows deep down that this is the end.

Then, all at once, we fell silent as the night. How any of us knew to stop making noises right at that moment, I have no idea, but the effect was so dramatic it made Nancarrow go quiet as well. And, as I watched, Vick leaned down and tugged the sack roughly off the bastard's head, leaving him blinking against the light, drips of piss still stuck to his eyelashes.

It must have taken a moment for his senses to adjust, because at first he just hung there, no longer screaming, no longer struggling, just staring and blinking. I was right about the gag, too. Someone had stuffed what appeared to be a rolled up pair of white underpants, complete with brown skid marks, right into his mouth, stretching it painfully wide. Beside me, one of the other Pigs moved away at that moment, heading for the corner of the barn, but I just watched the spectacle.

Vick crouched down next to Andy, and I reckon that's when the full magnitude of his situation dawned on him. His eyes rolled up to look at the figure bending down over him and his body started to rock and his hands scrabbled against the floor, trying to find any sort of hold. I couldn't blame him either, the sight of Vick, a bear of a man, looking like some sort of mythical pig-monster, muscles glistening with sweat and dick on full display, must have been a fucking shock to the system.

And, in that moment of shock, Vick grabbed a handful of the underpants-gag and ripped it right out of Nancarrow's mouth like it was some sort of magic trick, sending front teeth pinging into the air like popcorn kernels from a hot pan. Andy squealed and started to cry, Vick oinked, the rest of us grunted or oinked in response. The whole place was alive with sound.

As Andy was screeching for help from anyone who'd listen (nobody was), the Pig who'd left the group returned from the corner of the room with the longest fucking blade I've ever seen. It was some sort of poleaxe with a sharp-looking edge and a spike right above it, all attached to a long wooden pole. I had no idea what it was used for on a farm, if it was even a farm implement at all, but I could almost see the grin of approval on Vick's porcine face as he nodded and grabbed one of Andy's arms.

"What do you want?" Andy's face twisted in fear as he tried to keep his eyes on the sharp implement. He spoke in toothy, asthmatic words that spluttered and sprayed with phlegm and blood and snot and piss. "I'll tell you anything you need to know. Just stop!"

Nobody answered. Vick pinned his arm to the floor by the wrist, and as much as Andy squirmed and jerked and tried to yank his body away, it did no good. His other hand scrabbled against the floor and tried to slap Vick away, but it was like a fly knocking against a window.

"Stop! Please! I haven't done anything!"

Andy started screaming at that point, but it didn't do him any good. As the Pig with the poker grunted and oinked in excitement, he lined up the poleaxe blade with Andy's wrist, pinned in place by Vick. Then he raised it a little, nodded around at the rest of us, and brought it down with a dull thwack.

As Andy's screams were punctuated with sobs and gagging, I heard my stomach groan. But that hunger wasn't for meat or pigswill or any kind of food. It was for this. Pain. Blood. Fear. The smell of shit was palpable, and even though I couldn't see Nancarrow's backside I knew who was making it. The blade didn't go all the way through his wrist on that first attempt, either. I guess the bone stopped it in its tracks. The flesh was split and mangled, and blood poured out, but the axe was raised again and brought down with a sickening crunch.

Still, Andy's hand was attached to his arm, wordless screams ringing out across the barn. Some of those screams were mine, only they were more like piggy squeals of delight. And shit, I was already in deep enough. What harm would another step in that direction do?

I grabbed the poleaxe out of the other Pig's hands, and Vick looked up in my direction, and even past the pigskin I could tell that he was smiling like an indulgent parent.

"I know what this is about. It's about those fucking girls, right? You think I was the one . . . I wasn't. Fuck. No!" Andy's lips were turned down as he cried, blood trickling from the corner of his mouth, just as tears trickled from his eyes. "Please let me go home."

Vick, still pinning Andy's wrist in place, looked up at me. He nodded, and I aimed the blade, then lifted it and slammed it into the same mangled flesh of his wrist. There was a sound like wood splitting, followed by a *thunk* of metal against the bare earth as blood poured forth from both halves of Andy's arm.

The other Pigs let out squeals of pure pig-man delight and started jumping up and down and slamming their palms into their chests.

Vick oinked and grabbed at the bloody, slippery mess that was the wrist end of the severed hand. Once he'd got it in his grip, he dangled it above Andy's face, but the sicko was no longer looking. He was sobbing and moaning with the pain. But that didn't deter the rest of the Pigs, who grunted and snuffled and danced around their fallen prey. Vick passed the hand to one, then, one by one, they passed it around the group like a baton, and, every now and then, one of them would lean down right in Nancarrow's sobbing face and trail the sticky fingers over his flesh or mash the palm into his nose.

And hell, what was I going to do except join in? After all, it was me who severed the fucking thing. So, as I joined the victory dance with the rest of the Pigs, I started occasionally poking the bastard with the spiky bit of my poleaxe, in the sides or the leg or the crotch or the throat . . . basically anywhere that might be soft and painful.

"I'm sorry . . . I couldn't help it . . . " He rocked with his sobs, wincing at the pain, his voice distant and delirious. "Please . . . let me go. Please . . . "

Andy was a fighter when it came to holding onto his life, I'd give him that. Despite the loss of blood from the open, gaping wound that was making a mess of the floor, the nonce was gripping onto life and even consciousness. He was sobbing and begging us to let him go back home, as if lying in his own bed might somehow make everything better, when one of the Pigs appeared with a pair of old, rusty pliers, working the pincers in front of him with a click-click-click.

"It wasn't my fault . . . " Andy seemed to be muttering to himself at this point, which was probably for the best since nobody else cared. "Please."

The plier-wielding Pig dropped to his knees beside Andy and took a hold of his jaw with one hand, fingers sliding on the tears and phlegm and blood and piss. Andy clamped his mouth tight, pressing his lips together, shaking his head in some vain attempt to stop what was happening. And he must have known what was coming, because it didn't take a genius to work it out. But he really was in no state to resist. The Pig pressed the tip of the pliers against Andy's lips and pulled with his sliding fingers, and, as the sicko panted through his nose, blowing blood bubbles with every breath, his mouth was slowly, inexorably forced open.

Unable to pronounce the hard sounds, Andy moaned pathetically, eyes scanning the room for anyone who might take pity. "Nya . . . Nya . . . Shtoch . . . Cyees . . . "

The whole scene reminded me of a dentist from a horror movie operating on his unwilling patient. And the Pig, grunting and squealing, seemed to revel in the moment as he got those pliers right into Nancarrow's mouth before starting to fish around inside. The front teeth had already gone with the underpants-gag, but there were plenty more at the back, and he made no mistake about going right for them. In the pliers poked, and there was a grinding, clicking noise as he got them pinched in tight around one of those molars and then started jerking his arm back.

Andy screamed, the Pigs were scuffing and dancing and oinking, and I was still holding that fucking poleaxe like a kid with a red crayon. So, not to be outdone, I started cracking the blunt end of the axe against the floorboards to make a kind of drumbeat. And, as the first tooth pulled free with a kind of sucking sound, like when you get a welly stuck in mud, I clapped and squealed.

Slop, *sloop*, grunt, *oink, pop*. The Pig held a tooth aloft like it was fucking Excalibur or something. And the squeal that went up from the crowd—like it was feeding time at the trough or something.

Andy cried and squirmed and spat blood away, and his eyes scanned the gathered crowd. "They . . . fucking enjoyed it," he muttered. "Fucking whores."

That comment made the human part of me see red. Where he found the energy to be vile like that I have no idea, but it wasn't an advisable course of action. I mean, not a lot he could do at that point, and he must have known it, but he didn't make things any easier on himself. I felt the bile rise up inside my throat and the pig-energy start to flow. It was like the pigskin had fused itself to my soul, and like the berserkers of old I took on the spirit of the animal that donated its flesh. And maybe I took on a bit of my old man's spirit as well, seeing as it was his fucking mask. But, whatever the case, I felt that spirit inside me like I was taking one for the team and liking it, and that poleaxe in my hand suddenly felt real weighty.

With a squeal of piggy delight, I launched myself at Nancarrow, slamming the axe into his already tender flank. He screamed so hard I almost felt his pain, but I didn't give a shit. Ignoring the other Pigs around me, I drew back the axe, lined it up and took another pot shot. And another. And another, until eventually his screams stopped and all that was left was the dull thud, thwack of my axe chopping him clean in half.

***

A couple of the other Pigs wrapped the body in a plastic sheet, then hauled it out of the barn and headed out into one of the fields. As we stood under the cold showers, washing off the gore and dirt and sweat, Vick clapped me on the shoulder, and I could tell he was real proud of how I'd conducted myself.

"You did good, boy. If only your old man could have seen that. Next time, I'll show you where the bodies are buried, but for now you look exhausted."

I didn't answer. With the pigskin removed, cleaned and folded away neatly in its chest I no longer felt the fire in my belly I had felt before. In fact, I felt kind of cold, and not just from the chilly water pouring over my head.

After we'd all showered, hosed down the barn and dressed in our own clothes again, we all said our goodbyes, got in our cars and headed out away from Tremorn Farm, back to our regular, everyday lives as Hamford police officers. Some of the other guys were vaguely familiar once they had their clothes on, but I couldn't pick them out by name. Maybe that was also for another time. As for me, I'd worked up something of an appetite, so I headed downtown and grabbed drive-through, and ate it right there in the takeaway car park as I thought over what we'd done. I didn't really feel any regret over it, but it was a lot to take in. The whole thought of my dad doing the very same to some other poor fucker, and the number of bodies that might be buried out there, and whether I was going to take part again or just go back to my life, ran over and over in my mind.

Anyway, once the food was gone it was about two-thirty in the morning, and I thought I'd better make tracks back to Morwenna, catch some sleep before I had to get up for work and all that. So I made my way over there and tried to keep as quiet as I could when I slipped inside, and then made my way along the corridor to her bedroom.

As I passed Edward's room, something made me pause and look in, and there he was sleeping like a little angel in his bed, covers tucked up carefully by his mother, favourite teddy clutched in his arms.

I watched him like that for a long moment, thinking about myself as a kid and how I thought my dad, the policeman, would protect me from anything and everything. And now I was that policeman, and I was supposed to protect this little man from harm until he was old enough to look after himself. Hell, I was there to protect all the kids in Hamford, and the adults too. Anyone who might need someone to look out for them. And sure, it was a lot of responsibility on my head and shoulders, but it was an honour, too, and I never took it more seriously than I did right then.

"I'll keep you safe," I whispered, then rubbed my chin as my mind mulled over that thought.

Then I headed back to the front door, flicked the lock and double-checked that it was secure, then checked the windows in the living room and kitchen as well.

By the time I finally slipped quietly into bed beside Morwenna, another fifteen minutes had gone by while I double-checked power sockets and locks and windows, and she must have heard me moving around because she rolled over and laid an arm right across my chest.

"Did you bust some bad guys, babe?"

I nodded, though she didn't see it. Andy Nancarrow was a bad guy, one of the worst, and me and the rest of the Pigs busted him for sure. "We need to get me a key cut. I don't want you leaving the door unlocked anymore."

"Sure, whatever."

"I love you."

"Love you, too, silly. But I'm knackered, so you're not getting—"

I cut her off with a kiss; then we lay down together and I finally fell asleep.

THE WILLINGNESS OF PREY

PAUL ALLIH

"**N**ERVOUS, WILL?" ROMAN ASKED, SMIRKING.

Will cleared his throat for the obvious lie, and said, "No . . . No, why?"

Roman glanced to Camilla through the rearview as he steered the van on the dark, desolate road.

"No reason to be scared. Unless being scared gets your juices flowing more," Camilla said, a hint of seduction in her voice.

Camilla and Roman laughed.

Will forced himself to chuckle along, questioning what the hell he had gotten himself into.

He had been speaking to Camilla for a couple of months. They connected through a furry Facebook group. The two came together over their obsession with vore: the erotic fantasy of being consumed.

They started off exchanging their artwork of small, furry critters being eaten and digested by much larger, ravenous beasts. Will had always felt so alone in his morbid fascination, but finally meeting someone nearby with common appetites was akin to making a discovery.

Chatting through Facebook, they shared their desires and quickly became more personal. They exchanged phone numbers and spoke through texts. She made him aware of Roman, but the way she explained their relationship, it seemed like it was more of a father/daughter thing. It made sense. In pictures they didn't come off as a couple, either. Then there was the age gap. Roman was in his late fifties and Camilla was twenty. Camilla was a beautiful brunette; youthful and curves in all the right places. Model-hot, some would say. Roman looked like an old biker: haggard with leathery, sun-dried skin and grey, wiry hair and missing teeth. But Roman's passive-aggressive demeanor left Will to wonder.

Maybe they were a couple?

It would answer for why she only wanted to speak through texts. It would also account for why it took so long for them to meet in the flesh. One time she fell ill. Then she had to cancel because her brother dropped by unexpectedly. Then she had to watch her sister's kids because her sister was going into labor with child number five and the dad had fled. All those red flags he tried his damnedest to ignore over the past few weeks were becoming brighter and more apparent.

"How much further is it?" Will asked, trying to play it cool, and casual.

Maneuvering a huge dip with the van, Roman responded with not much of an answer, "A little bit down the way."

When Camilla agreed to meet Will at FurKis, the local furry convention, he thought that was it. He was finally going to get closer to the pretty girl who shared so many of his interests. Some so outlandish that he tended to feel alone. They agreed to meet in the back lot of the convention center at 6 pm. She would make it this time, she promised.

There was Will, dressed to the neck as his squirrel-self, holding his head in his hands. It was fifteen after six and he was questioning whether or not Camilla decided to ditch him at the last minute. Then that big, black panel van rolled into the parking lot. It pulled up in front of him and Camilla hopped out of the passenger door in her human form. Roman's face was lit up with that smile of his from the driver's seat. Camilla begged Will to hop inside. She lured him with the promise of something unforgettable—something he'd been wanting.

He had his reservations, but he couldn't resist her. Even with that strange old man and his devil-grin behind the wheel of his blackened Caravan, he couldn't turn her down. He was under her spell.

Camilla rubbed on Will's furry shoulder.

"I know you had your heart set on the convention, Will, but this is going to be much better. Trust me."

Will didn't know what they had in store for him. For all he knew, they were taking him out to the middle of nowhere and robbing him. Or worse. His mind was running wild and he was pouring sweat into his fur suit.

"We'll have to go to the next one," Will said, clinging to his headgear for dear life.

Roman shook his head, disgusted.

"Yeah, well, you two have fun palling around with the self-righteous asshats that run that place."

Will looked at Roman with confusion, and Camilla explained.

"Roman was asked to leave the last FurKis after he got into an argument with the organizer and his girlfriend. They accused him of being . . . what was it, Roman?"

"They said I was toxic," Roman said, smugly. "They're delusional. They think they can Disney up our shit and drive out anyone who isn't ashamed to hide their kinks, and for what? So, the media doesn't mock us? It's BS. Even if we don't give those vultures ammunition, they just make up the shit anyway . . . "

Roman gave a soft slap across Will's shoulder, causing Will to flinch.

"Hey Will, did you hear about that furry orgy where a brother unknowingly impregnated his sister while they were both in costume?"

"I think remember that."

"BS! And the yiffing fest that broke out at a midnight showing of Zootopia? Ya hear about that one?"

Will nodded again.

"That was BS, too," Roman said. "See, it's all about clicks and ads. They don't give a damn about what community they hurt or who they damage, so why should we care about how they view us?"

Camilla rolled her eyes and groaned.

"Oh, Roman, just calm down. Don't ruin our night with your ranting." Leaning forward, she ran her fingers through the shaggy hair on Will's head; suggestively massaging his scalp from the back to the front. "Will here is just along for a good time, and he doesn't want to hear this nastiness. Isn't that right Will?"

Torn by liking the sensations Camilla was giving him and the glare he was feeling from Roman; Will shrugged sheepishly.

"I don't mind," Will said, staying neutral. "It's your van, so do what you want. You know?"

Roman pulled out his vape and took a long, deep hit while shooting Camilla a dirty look through the rearview. He shook his head and exhaled a large cloud. The scent of Fruity Pebbles filled the air as an awkward silence fell over the interior.

Will didn't know if it was being told in so many words to shut up or Camilla's playing with his hair, but Roman looked pissed off. He still wasn't sure of their relationship. There hadn't been any physical contact between them, but they interacted like an old married couple. Sniping and glaring at one another, just like his parents.

"So," Will said, squirming away from Camilla's pleasuring long nails. "How much further do we have to go?"

Letting her dejection be known, Camilla huffed loudly and plopped back in her seat.

"We're here," Roman said.

Roman spun the wheel, turning off the road and onto a narrow, gravely path. About a half mile or so up the trail, Will saw the outline of a two-story house and what looked like a big barn behind it. There wasn't much light around the property, and it was surrounded by tall trees and bushy shrubs.

Roman snickered. "Get ready to slip into your furs, Ladies."

***

With his headgear on, Will's fursona, Raquel Red-Squirrel had come out to play.

Raquel Red-Squirrel was fiery auburn with a white belly who rocked an oversized, pink bow on top of her head with big tail bouncing behind her. She was a Southern firecracker who was everything Will wished he was: up-beat, confident, and oozing sexual energy. She didn't shy away from anyone or anything, and she exuded that in her give-no-fucks strut, moving behind Camilla.

Camilla's fursona was Chanel; a fluffy, grey-and-white chinchilla fixed with a big white cloth diaper around her bushy tail. The baby girl with attitude kept glancing back at Will through her big, sweet cartoon eyes, enamored with his transformation.

They followed Roman's fursona, Rasputin. A rat; his rodent was wise and fatherly. He was almost diabolical looking, with burning red eyes that seemed to shine from his shaggy, black hair. His tail was long and gray, and he had pointy buck teeth and sharp claws. He led them to a large, square, concrete building on a hill hundreds of yards behind the house. It was tall and wide, like a warehouse. It had doors, but it didn't appear to have any windows.

The large, cold structure would have been ominous to Will. But Will wasn't there at the moment. It was Raquel Red-Squirrel, and nothing would bring harm to that spunky gal.

"Are you gonna show us your big, long jet plane, Roman?" Will said, teasingly, in Raquel's over-the-top southern belle twang.

"No, Will," Roman said with a chuckle. "This isn't a hangar."

"Uh, Honey—do you see anything resembling a man on me?"

"No?"

"Now then, you will call me Raquel or Ms. Red-Squirrel; do we understand each other?"

"Yes, Ma'am. My deepest apologies."

"You can call me, Ma'am. I like the way that sounds coming from you."

"Yes, Ma'am."

Camilla laughed and cooed.

Roman slid off his glove and stepped up to the tall double-doors. He punched his code into the lighted keypad and the doors unlatched with a loud click. Pushing them open, Roman flipped the lights on and walked inside. He made his way up to a large object covered by a giant tarp as the fluorescents flickered on to display a clean, high-tech machine shop: air compressors, drill presses, and lathes and computers.

"I've been working on this non-stop for five years. Some would call me insane, but fuck 'em if they don't get it."

Tugging off the tarp, Roman unveiled a giant, robotic snake.

It laid flat; the head and the neck and part of the stomach. It was on a platform, propped up five feet off the ground with tubes and wires going into it. It was made of steel and heavy latex for skin. The head was the size of a compact car and shaped like an arrowhead. Its body was about the length of a school bus, but much skinnier and its green, reptilian skin was speckled with white and yellow dots.

"What is it?" Will asked, amazed but confused.

"It's a Green Tree Python," Roman answered, going to a laptop.

"I mean, what does it do?"

"Watch . . . "

Roman's fingers tapped upon the keys of his computer, and with the hissing of hydraulics and winding of gears, the snake came to life. Its eyes lit up red and its mouth opened; its jaws unlocked and slowly widened. Large, chrome fangs shot outwards and gleamed beneath the lights while its lower jaw continued to extend. Descending lower and lower, it almost touched the floor before finally stopping, exposing a row of smaller teeth along the outer rim on each side, jagged like saw blades.

Awestruck, Will plucked off his mask and staggered towards the magnificent machine.

"You built this? he gasped.

"That's right," Roman said, pride in his voice. "I spent the better part of my existence working for Disney, making this kind of stuff."

Turning to Roman, Will questioned him with child-like wonder, "So, you just lie inside and the jaws close in around you?"

"Yeah. It's big enough to cradle Shaq in there. The tongue is pretty much a twin mattress covered with red, rubber sheets: soft and squishy. There are nozzles in there that mist with vapor for the effect of saliva. It's not as realistic as it would have been with water, but the water was just too messy, but that's not all . . . keep looking . . . "

Will walked around the snake, taking it in. His eyes growing wider and his mouth becoming more agape as Roman further explained his creation.

"A conveyer belt slowly rolls you down into the mid-section: its stomach, and you can rest inside. Like you were digested."

Camilla saw the look of excitement on Will's face.

"It's like a dream come true, isn't it?"

Catching his breath, Will replied, "I just can't believe it."

Since he could remember, he had always wanted to know what it would feel like. His tiny, frail rodent body lying in the mouth of a salivating predator. Coaxed down its gully and worked into its gut, where he'd be nestled. Cradled in absolute warmth, becoming one with the hungry beast. The thought made him tingle all over. He was always convinced it was impossible, but there he was face-to-face with a machine that could make his fantasies come true. He could swear he was dreaming.

"Enough talking about it," Roman said. "How about we see what it can do?"

After some quick finger work on his computer, Roman grabbed a step ladder and brought it over to the snake. He placed it in front of the mouth and slid his rat mitt back on. Gingerly, he climbed up the ladder in his bulky rat suit, and slowly crawled into the snake's gaping jaws.

Lying down, he got comfortable while he explained.

"The program is set up to run itself. You just have to pick the setting, 'auto-mode', hit enter and it should do all the work from there."

He lay there, waiting, but nothing happened.

"Any second now," he said, nervously waiting for it to work.

Then the mechanisms started moving.

"There we go!"

Will and Camilla watched as the mouth began to close. It started off slow, then quickly clamped shut and a painful wail echoed from the mouth of the contraption. Then it opened, then snapped closed again, repeating; chomping down on Roman with power of hydraulics in the jaws. His bones crunched as the teeth sliced through his flesh. His screams were a strange mixture of pleasure and pain. Joyous howls shifted to bawls of torture as blood ran from sides of the snake's mouth and dripped to the concrete floor.

Will whipped around to Camilla.

"Is this supposed to happen?"

Camilla didn't say a word. She just watched.

The jaws opened, and Roman's right arm slid out. Before he could draw it back, the mouth closed again, chomping down on his furry limb. The blades cut and ground, severing it mid-forearm as Roman shrieked. The paw tumbled down the side and dropped to the floor, plopping into an expanding puddle of crimson. Roman was writhing. There was no pleasure in his cries. He was dying; kicking and screaming with thuds and bangs from inside his mechanical tomb.

"We have to *do* something!" Will hollered at Camilla.

Camilla shook her head, 'no'. Her big, cartoon eyes and her goofy smile beneath her rosy, red cheeks made her reaction all the more off-putting.

"This is why we're here," Camilla said, hauntingly.

He didn't have time to question her or dissect her words. Frantic,

Will ran to the laptop. With his heart pounding, he threw off his mitts, and he tried to click out of the program. He was swiping and clicking but it wasn't doing anything. Taking a deep breath, he counted back from ten, and worked to clear his head. All he could think about was being arrested and charged with murder. He couldn't shake the feeling that he was an accessory. He closed his eyes to the bloodshed and attempted to block out the agonizing wails that filled the warehouse. *Think, damn it, think!*

The mechanical python made a new sound. The red-splattered mouth closed tight, and the hydraulics started pumping while the gears churned in its guts.

"What's happening now?"

"It's digesting him," Camilla said, joyously.

***

Roman's bloodied body was carried slowly into the belly of his death machine. So far, it had worked as intended. No matter how much he anticipated it, he couldn't fully prepare himself for the pain he would feel. His bones were cracked and shattered; his organs were lacerated and punctured. It was becoming harder to breathe and voluntary movement was non-existent. His mask had been taken from his head at some point and his suit was ruptured. The remaining shreds of his fur were smashed and matted into his mangled flesh.

Pain was the whole of the experience; the shock and the unexpected fury of being gnashed and chomped for sustenance. The sensation of being crunched and chewed before ultimately being swallowed had been Roman's fantasy since he was a boy, and this was the realization of his dream.

***

Thinking fast, Will saw a fire axe in a case on the wall to his left. He waddled over to it and smashed the glass out of the case with a few jabs from his elbow. Ripping the axe out of the broken case, he charged towards the mid-section of the snake as fast as the lower half of his costume would allow.

Seeing what Will was up to, Camilla rushed to him. Just as he drew the axe back, Camilla threw her shoulder into his side as hard as she could. She knocked him to the ground and her head popped off and tumbled away. The axe went sliding across the floor. Will

55

tried to get up, but Camilla pounced on him and pinned his shoulders.

"Get off! I've got to help him!" Will shouted, his face beet-red as he fought to get up.

"No," Camilla grunted, pushing down on Will as hard as she could. "I can't let you do that!"

"If he dies, we're murderers, and I ain't a fucking murderer!"

Pressing down harder, Camilla screamed in his face, "He made me promise, and I gave him my word! And I'm not breaking my word!"

***

Roman's ride stopped with a jerk, jarring his battered shell. He winced from the discomfort and prepared himself. Three rows of tiny sprayers above him came on. They were misting like sprinklers inside a greenhouse; moistening. The drizzle falling upon him was a hybrid of acids. The carefully chosen concoction was dangerous to human flesh, but it was safe for plastics and metals. It would act like stomach acids, dissolving him slowly, as if he were actually being secreted into the belly of a large, hungry serpent.

At first, it was hard to tell if the acids were working. The spray was light, and with the other sensations that were tremoring through his body, Roman's nerve endings were already working overtime. Then one of the sprayers malfunctioned. Its tip popped off and the fluid poured like a small faucet. It came down onto his forehead and ran over his face and the burning was undeniable.

At first, it felt like little pinches in his pores, and then came the searing as the chemicals burned off the layers of skin and worked through the muscles and tendons, slowly turning them into a pulpy gelatin. He screamed and hollered as his nose was reduced into a messy clump of pink; foaming and steaming as cartilage smoldered. Another nozzle went and then another, and then another. Thick, concentrated streams were gushing all over him. Splashing over his arms and torso, and his stomach and thighs. Softening the meat and the bits of fur into mush; bubbling and sizzling to the bones.

Thick clouds of smoke were billowing up around him. Something was wrong with the machine. The acid was eating through the metal, but that couldn't be right. Did he miscue the mixture? Did he use the wrong type somewhere along the way? Roman couldn't be certain, but there was nothing he could do about it. His concerns about his beloved device were about as useless as his feeble shell. Numbness washed over him, and his sight fluttered before going to black.

***

Camilla kept all her weight on Will.

"This is what he wanted, and I'm going next. I thought you wanted this, too."

There was a loud pop and Will's eyes shot to the platform. Smoke was pouring out from between the machine and its components.

"Look," he shouted, his bulging eyes fixed on the snake.

Seeing the panic on his face, Camilla looked to the snake. Smoke and sparks took her attention.

Will came up from the ground and backed away towards the only way out. Following a loud pop, there was hissing and screeching. Sparks suddenly flared into flames and they started spreading up from the bottom of the snake.

Camilla just stared as the once magnificent creation broke down into ruins. Like her once strong, vibrant person who was trapped inside of its belly. Everything she had ever known was right there, slowly smoldering before her. She'd met Roman at a diner outside of Orlando while she was panhandling. She was sixteen. Her father, she never knew, and her mother was a drunk who had thrown her out onto the streets. She had no one. Roman took her in. He became her caregiver. He helped her discover her fursona. No one saw him the way she did. Their bond was something special. A once-in-a-lifetime kind of love; a love that was too much for this world.

Will shouted, "Come on: we gotta get out of here!"

The flames expanded, engulfing the snake. Its eyes blinked, and sparks shot from its jittering jaws. There was a loud bang and the robot crashed through the platform, causing the fire to spread out. The flames grew higher; inching towards the ceiling while creeping to the walls. The building was turning into a kiln, and there was no stopping it. All they could do was flee.

Will grabbed Camilla by her arm and snatched her out of her daze. Self-preservation kicked in, and she ran with him to the doors. Waddling as fast as they could while the machinery crumbled and broke apart in a roaring inferno.

THE WILLINGNESS OF PREY

***

Will kept running down the hill; Camilla stopped and turned.

Catching her breath, her gaze fixed on the warehouse as smoke rose from the roof and poured from the doors. Her eyes watered; her heart weighed heavy. She was supposed to have gone after him, but there she was; alive and alone.

Will slowed to a halt and turned back to Camilla. He stomped to her, seething and out of breath.

"What the fuck was that, huh?!"

Camilla wiped the tears from her eyes and looked to Will.

"I wanted to give you something that few would ever experience. Our fantasies lived out."

Will gawked at her as if she had sprouted a second head.

"We just watched a man kill himself!"

"And that's how he wanted to end it!"

Will knew it was true. As disturbing as the whole scene was, Roman hoisted himself into the mouth of his creation and offered himself as a meal. No one forced him, and no one tricked him into doing it.

"I thought you were into vore?" Camilla questioned. "The images were all over your profile; your drawings of you, Raquel Red-Squirrel, being eaten and swallowed. The ones you made for me. Remember, all those conversations we had? You told me all about how you wished you could be eaten? Devoured, you said. I thought I was giving you something special. Or were those lies?"

"I wasn't lying, I . . . "

"You what?! I saw how excited you were when you saw Roman's machine. You looked like a kid on Christmas morning. You wanted to get inside, just like me. I could see it in your eyes!"

"I did, but that was before," Will said, his anger waning as his nausea grew, thinking back to the blood and the screams. The sounds of Roman's body breaking and the smell of his flesh searing; his burnt fur.

"Watching him die in that thing . . . it terrified me," Will confessed. "Even if it didn't burst into flames, I don't think I could do it. I guess I'm not the prey I thought I was."

Seeing how shaken and vulnerable he was, Camilla went to Will. She put her arms around his waist and squeezed.

"Believe it or not, I was scared, too. I don't think I was ready. Not like Roman. He's gone now, and that's what he wanted."

Will's arms draped over Camilla. He was unsure at first, but when he felt her nestle closer, he began to hold her tight. She was just like him; weakened and exposed, and, like him, she was all alone. She needed him like he needed her. They basked in their embrace and watched the warehouse burn.

6 DICKS

RACHEL LEE WEIST

"**OH, I'VE GOT SOMETHING** for you, all right," Sloan said, tapping a cigarette from the pack and clamping it between his yellowed fangs. With a flick of his silver lighter, the coyote leaned across the glass jewelry case and exhaled a stream of noxious smoke, his gold tooth glittering under the fluorescent lighting of Sloan's Porn Emporium. "I've got something in the back you've never *seen*."

"Show me," said Wax. The opossum wrung his paws in anticipation and stepped towards the counter, careful not to take his eyes off Sloan.

Toenails clicking on the tile, Sloan wove through the aisles of latex, leather, and silicone to the storefront. After locking the door and switching the sign from open to closed, Sloan bent to pluck a ribbed green phallus from the floor and returned it to the window display, where a multi-colored forest of dildos stood erect on a dusty satin sheet. Clapping his paws together, Sloan rejoined Wax and parted the bead curtain leading to the rear of the store.

"After you," Sloan said.

Wax shook his head. After a long moment, Sloan grinned.

Sloan led Wax through a dim hallway to the back room, unlocked a metal door, and continued down a short flight of stairs into the basement. The mingled scent of blood, sweat, and ejaculate lay thick in the humid air. The basement housed a pair of stainless-steel tables, a workstation with a sewing machine, and a collection of tools that Wax couldn't identify; however, it was the suit hanging on the far wall that drew the possum's attention. Wax's mouth flooded with saliva. A string of drool dangled from his needle-like teeth, and Wax wiped it away, realizing with embarrassment that Sloan had been watching. He flushed at the sound of the coyote's wheezing laughter.

"You like what you see."

It was not a question. In Sloan's line of work, statements sold more sex than questions. Unable to shift his gaze from Sloan's glorious creation, Wax realized that he had lost sight of the coyote. Two paws settled on Wax's shoulders and squeezed. Wax jumped but was too awestruck to flee.

His voice a whisper, Wax said, "Can I touch one?"

"You must," Sloan said. "I insist."

Wax inspected the suit, pinching and rubbing the supple pink material in his paw. The suit was fitted for animals with specialized tastes—beasts who preferred to walk and fuck on all fours, instead of walking on their hind legs like civilized animals.

Wax had never been attracted to the idea of walking on all fours, preferring his front paws soft and well-manicured, but would debase himself in a heartbeat for an opportunity to wear the smooth suit. Or, better yet, to sample a taste of what it would be like to fuck a human, zipping some anonymous dumpster-critter into the suit and humping her to completion, stroking the hairless skin with his eyes closed.

Sloan cleared his throat.

"Shit," Wax said. While fantasizing, Wax's paw had crept to the crotch of his tailored slacks and was massaging his stiff penis. A wet spot had darkened the fabric, and the opossum angled his hips away from the coyote in embarrassment

"Occupational hazard," Sloan said. He lit a second cigarette off the cherry of his first and stamped the expired butt out in a crystal ashtray.

"You own a fuck shop; you meet a lot of dicks." Sloan slipped Wax a wink.

Wax tried to laugh, but his mouth had gone dry. He was filled with a sudden desperation, a sinking feeling in his gut, and he asked the question before he could lose his nerve. "How much?"

Sloan straightened his spine and swaggered to the wall of suits. "This baby is hand-made, one-of-a-kind, designed by yours truly. I call it a 'silkie.' You won't find anything like it on the market."

The coyote spun on his paw and walked the length of the wall.

"Top of the line materials, organic, custom-fitted to the buyer upon purchase. Rare." Sloan paused, locked eyes with Wax, and said, "Expensive."

The opossum sagged, staring at the suit with longing.

"There are other ways to pay," Sloan said.

Wax sensed a trap, then decided the reward was worth the risk. "Tell me."

Sloan stood back from the wall and put a paw on Wax's shoulder. They gazed at the suits together. "Resource acquisition," the coyote said. "The suit material is hard to cum by—pun intended."

Without waiting for Wax to react, Sloan said, "I'll cut you a deal if you procure your own materials. You bring me what I need, I'll make you what you need. Agreed?"

"Fine, yes," Wax said. He took the coyote's extended paw and shook it. "Anything."

Sloan chuckled. The coyote said, "It's human dick skin."

Wax frowned. "What?"

"Guy your size, I figure you'll need six dicks if you want a full body suit. Maybe just five if you lose a few pounds. You bring me the skin; I'll make you the suit."

"Where am I supposed to get something like that?"

"South of the belly button; north of the knees. You'll figure it out."

#1

Wax trundled through side alleys, head whirling with possible plans and scenarios. The goal was simple: find a human male, kill him, and get the precious skin to Sloan.

The opossum heard voices approaching and crouched behind a dumpster, recalling the human aversion to clothed animals and trying to avoid harassment. The streetlight cast unusual shadows on the surrounding brick walls.

A bearded man was stumbling down the alley, supported by an overweight bald man on the right and a lanky man with shaggy brown hair on the left. The drunken man began to sing a shanty song in a deep, booming voice, bellowing laughter. Wax heard the bald man say, "Get it together. We're here."

The trio halted outside a painted red door set in the side of the brick building, and Wax swallowed a lump in his throat, his paw flying to the pepper spray in his pocket.

"Hang on." The ruddy-cheeked, bearded man slurred his words, removing a flask from inside his jacket pocket. He took a long pull from the flask, belched, and said, "Put some more hair on my chest."

"Brian, if you're not going to take this seriously, then get lost. Don't embarrass us," said the lanky man.

"Okay, o-kay," the bearded drunk said. He raised his hands in defense. "Meet you inside. I need a smoke first."

"Jesus Christ," said the bald man, shaking his head. He knocked on the door, a hatch slid open, and he slipped a card of stationary through the hatch to the other side. The red door creaked open, releasing a blast of loud music. Wax watched laser lights dancing on the brick outside before the door slammed shut.

The bearded drunkard staggered several yards in Wax's direction, slumped against the alley wall and fumbled a cigarette into his mouth. After a couple of long drags, he bent double, vomited a cocktail of beer and liquor on his leather boots, and tumbled head-first into a heap of black garbage bags.

It would be easy, Wax thought, to kill the unconscious man lying in the garbage pile. He lifted a long shard of green glass from a broken bottle beneath the dumpster, used a candy wrapper to form a handle, and sneaked across the alley.

But, how to go about it? Stabbing would wake the man, and Wax doubted the glass would pierce the man's leather jacket. The throat, then.

Wax pressed the piece of glass to the man's throat, where he thought the artery should be. Averting his eyes, Wax gripped the handle with both paws, shifted his weight forward and slashed. The glass parted the man's skin with ease but failed to sever the artery. The drunkard stirred in his sleep, and Wax began to panic. The opossum sawed at the man's throat with long, hard strokes, adrenaline pounding in his ears, as he tried to remember where the humans kept their arteries. When he cut into the man's windpipe, the drunkard finally came to, thrashing and attempting to scream through the blood flooding his lungs.

"Shit," Wax said, abandoning the slashing and stabbing the glass into the side of the drunkard's neck. The man clutched at the glass and yanked it free. Blood jetted from the wound, soaking Wax in steaming gouts, and the opossum recoiled in horror. Within seconds, the man stopped moving. Wax felt thick, hot fluids pooling between his toes and climbed onto the garbage bags to avoid the disgusting mess, poking at the dripping corpse.

The opossum, driven by the fear of being caught, retrieved the metal lid of an overturned garbage can and placed it over the corpse's head, hiding the man's glassy eyes from view. Wax tore holes in the surrounding garbage bags, pawed the refuse over the drunkard's dead form, and sat panting atop the layer of trash.

***

It was after midnight when Wax pounded on the door to Sloan's apartment, located above the sex shop, and the coyote cracked the door without unlocking the chain. The metallic glint of a revolver barrel shone in the darkness. Sloan released a menacing growl, his nose twitching at the smell of gore. He said, "What the *fuck* do you want?"

"I did it," Wax said, looking over his shoulder to ensure no one was listening in. "I got you one of them."

Sloan grunted and began to shut the door.

"Wait!" Wax's words came spilling forth as, excited, the opossum attempted to recount the night's events before Sloan could shut him out.

When he had finished, Sloan slid back the chain and opened the door. The coyote stared at Wax, expressionless. In a flat tone he said, "You killed the guy."

"Yeah," Wax said, puzzled. "Just like you said."

"I never said to kill anybody," Sloan said. He shook his head and rubbed the back of his neck, scratching behind his ear. "Goddamnit. Okay, so where's the dick then? Hand it over."

"I thought—"

"You didn't think, or we'd be having this conversation during business hours, and I'd have a dick in my hand. Why the hell didn't you just cut it off and let the freak go?"

"But—"

"Go get the dick. Bring it here tomorrow, then bring me five more. Now get the fuck off my porch."

The door slammed shut, leaving the opossum to slink back to his quarry and harvest the organ.

***

Wax spent the next day strategizing. Every few hours, he masturbated with frantic urgency, thinking of the silkie suit for motivation.

He was a small animal and, while his teeth were sharp, Wax was not built for strength. This presented serious issues for the aspiring dick-thief. He sat at the chipped Formica table in his studio apartment, scrawling ideas in a notepad. When a cockroach skittered across the table, Wax's paw darted out to snatch the insect, and he popped it into his mouth, savoring the crunch between his teeth as the juices wet his tongue. Wax smacked his lips in satisfaction.

The list of ideas grew longer.

#2

Wax returned to the red door in the brick alleyway. The alley had been cleared of garbage and the blood washed away, presumably after the drunkard's body was reported, and Wax was surprised to find that the murder had not affected the club's business. It was a Saturday night, and the alley was teeming with various attendees. When a slender young woman, wearing tight, zebra-striped leggings and a tube top, separated from the crowd with a tanned, muscular man in tow, the opossum stalked the pair for three blocks to an abandoned warehouse—a popular location for nefarious activity—and watched through a window as the woman dropped to her knees and unbuckled the man's belt.

She slipped her hand into the man's designer jeans and pulled forth a pink cock, sliding it between her painted lips and swallowing its length. The man moaned, pumping his hips.

When he climaxed, the man's dick popped free from the woman's lips, squirting cum on her cheeks and down her sequined tube top. With a coy smile, the woman wiped the fresh semen from her face and poked her fingers into her mouth to suck them clean; however, as she discovered the extent of the mess, the woman scowled and said, "Fred, you son-of-a-bitch, this top is brand new."

The man shrugged. He said, "There's a sink in the back, go get cleaned up. I'll be ready for round two when you get back."

"There won't be a round two," the woman said over her shoulder, her ass jiggling as she strolled across the warehouse. The man said, "We'll see."

Nervous, Wax slid a straight razor from his pocket—a gift from Sloan after the coyote had received the drunkard's dick, its base sawed ragged from the piece of glass. Wax hoisted himself through an open window and dropped to the cement floor behind the unsuspecting man.

The man was preparing himself to fuck by rubbing the head of his dick and stroking the shaft, his expensive watch rattling as his hand picked up speed. Bleached-blond hair, lightly gelled, flopped into the man's eyes, and he tossed his head to clear his vision.

At the sound of approaching footsteps, Wax leapt between the man's legs and swiped the straight razor overhead, severing the dick with a single stroke. As blood showered from the open wound, Wax waited for the dick to flop to the ground. It didn't; instead, the dick remained clutched in the man's fist, far out of the opossum's reach.

The man began to scream. In response, the woman came running from the bathroom, rushing towards her bleeding companion. Without hesitation, she punted Wax like a football. The opossum sailed through the air and struck the wall behind the screaming man, the straight razor spinning across the concrete as the woman slipped in her companion's blood, lost her balance, and fell hard on her back. The man swayed on his feet, succumbing to blood loss, and finally dropped his dick in an attempt to staunch the bleeding with his hands.

Wax gasped for air. He scampered over the woman, clawing her face, and skidded through the pool of blood, scooping up the dick with his paws. Wax hurried to retrieve the straight razor and caught sight of the glow from the woman's cell phone as she called 9-1-1. Ignoring the burning in his lungs, Wax bolted for the window and—fueled by adrenaline—leapt clean through the opening, leaving a trail of bloody footprints in his wake.

***

The bells dangling from the front door of Sloan's shop jingled, announcing the freshly washed opossum's arrival with the severed dick secreted in a small black bag from the liquor store. Wax approached the coyote with apprehension.

Sloan was focused on the small flat screen television mounted on the wall behind the counter. Without shifting his gaze from the "Breaking News" bulletin, Sloan said, "You have got to be the dumbest, no-brain-having motherfucker."

Ducking his head, Wax dropped the black bag on the glass counter and wrung his hands.

"You made the news, asshole." Sloan gestured at the television and said, "Lucky for you, the bitch who called the cops was cum-drenched and high as a kite, otherwise you'd be looking at a city-wide 'possum hunt."

"They said all that on the news?" Wax frowned and stared at the screen, incredulous. Although the city was rife with crime, cum-drenched and drug-fueled reports of cock abduction seemed like a risqué subject, even for Channel 9 news.

Sloan pinched the bridge of his nose and shook his head. "I have eyes and ears all over the city. There were about twenty-five rats living in that warehouse, where you decided to throw your little party, and I swear if—"

The rest of the coyote's words deteriorated into a litany of growled curses.

Wax felt a sinking sensation in his chest. He said, "Does this mean you won't make the suit anymore?"

"No, I'll make it. But after this is all over, if you somehow manage to pull it off, you are going to owe me—*really* owe me. Consider this practice, because you're going full-time into the dick-thieving business for the rest of your miserable, flea-ridden life." Sloan loomed over Wax, eyes narrowed to thin, menacing slits, and he said, "You sure you want that kind of debt hanging over your head?"

Wax shuffled his feet and glanced at the bead curtain behind Sloan. "Can I touch the suit again?"

3, # 4

With the members of the nightclub on high alert, Wax was forced to hunt elsewhere. Heeding a strict warning from Sloan, the opossum was careful to avoid the inner city, choosing instead to scout the rest stop on the city's outer edge.

The rest stop had fallen into disrepair, following the construction of the new bridge and the redirected highway. Wax padded across the cracked pavement of the parking lot, with its faded white lines, towards the tan brick box of the restrooms. He was not concerned with being seen—a single functioning streetlamp clung to life, a blinking dull orange that failed to illuminate the sidewalk below. The lawn was overgrown with tall weeds, and the trees covered with twisted strands of ivy.

Wax was seeking a lone vagrant, but the homeless people squatting in the woods beyond the blackberry bushes traveled in groups. Disheartened, the opossum trudged back towards the parking lot, sinking deep into the knowledge that he might never feel the constricting caress of the silkie suit stretched tight over his body; might never sink his pink dick into the pussy of another opossum and pretend he was fucking a human woman.

Twin headlights swept over the wall of the restrooms. A semi truck rumbled into the parking lot and hissed to a stop, shiny black door swinging open.

Startled, Wax darted into the men's restroom: a two-stalled facility that reeked of piss and clogged toilets. A single discarded boot lay on its side below the restroom sink, torn and lying in a pool of brown water. Wax ran past the boot. He skidded under the door of the bathroom stall and leapt up onto the toilet. Perched on the toilet seat, the opossum found himself eye-level with a doorknob-sized hole cut through to the adjoining stall.

A strange idea sparked in his mind. The opossum listened for footsteps and decided to take the risk, ducking under the stall again and retrieving the soggy boot. He positioned the boot where it would be visible from the adjoining stall and, by standing on the toilet seat, was able to reach across the tiny space to lock the door.

The odds were slim that events would progress as planned, but the restroom was dark, and the edges of the glory hole were smooth—well-used. Wax heard the truck driver's heavy footfalls enter the bathroom. In the darkness, Wax could make out the man's hat over the top of the stall, and the truck driver jiggled the lock. Improvising, Wax grunted.

"Shit, sorry," the truck driver said. His shoes thudded into the next stall and the lock clicked shut.

Another grunt, and Wax pulled at the laces of the old boot, managing to tap it against the floor. Hoping to attract the truck driver's attention to the glory hole, Wax knocked three times on the adjoining wall. The opossum's heart leapt in his chest when he saw the vague shape of a man's finger tracing the rim of the hole, and he heard the truck driver's stream of piss slow, then drip to a stop.

The truck driver said, "Is that what you're into, buddy? You want some of this?"

Wax chewed his lip and decided that a moan was a satisfactory response.

"Alright, you asked for it," said the truck driver.

A dark shape pushed through the hole, poking Wax in the nose before he could react to the surprising length. Compared to the previous two, the shadow-dick was an anaconda.

Although Wax was impressed by his own improvisation, the plan's progress was beginning pick up speed, threatening to derail at the slightest misstep. Afraid to touch the massive dick with his tiny, sharp-clawed paws, Wax screwed up his face in disgust and licked the tip of the truck driver's dick, hoping the man wouldn't detect the raspy nature of his tongue. In response, the truck driver moaned and pushed the dick further through the hole.

Wax spit salty pre-cum into the toilet bowl, placed the blade of the straight razor flush with the stall wall—like a miniature guillotine—and delivered a quick slice to the base of the truck driver's shaft; however, the girth was too thick for the blade to pass through completely, and Wax gaped in confusion as the dick dangled, three-quarters detached, over the lip of the glory hole. He was not good at this, Wax decided, as he sank his tiny claws into the head of the dick and leapt from the toilet seat. The opossum's weight stretched the attached skin tight over the hole's rim and, when the skin tore free, he felt his paws fall flat on the ground.

The wall of the bathroom stall vibrated with the truck driver's roar. The injured man, fueled by rage, kicked open the door to Wax's stall. He bent, seized the opossum, and Wax felt his spine being twisted in the man's rough hands. Terrified, Wax clung to the dick, sunk his fangs into the man's hand and felt the truck driver's grip loosen. The opossum fled from the restroom, pursued by the truck driver, and dove into the blackberry bushes, burrowing deep despite the thorns scraping his skin. Behind him, Wax heard the man's thundering voice diminish as, crashing through the brush in pursuit, the truck driver collapsed unconscious.

Wax emerged into the homeless camp, his forward momentum nearly spilling him into the campfire where a group of six sat gaping at the dick—still leaking blood—cradled in the opossum's furry clutches.

He spent the night in a tree, cold, with the dick in a bag hanging from a nearby branch.

***

Sloan led Wax into the basement, where the coyote was hard at work on the silkie suit. A bottle of scotch and an overflowing ashtray were positioned beside the sewing machine. A scalpel sat on one of the steel tables in a drizzle of blood. Sloan indicated the pink dick lying on the table's surface, saying, "I figured you ought to see how the sausage is made, so to speak."

The coyote chuckled at the poor joke. He placed the dick in the bottom of a dissection tray and ran a scalpel the length of the shaft, parting the delicate skin with ease. Sloan folded the dick open to expose the spongy tissue within and used pins to secure the flesh to the tray. Like a trapper cleaning a pelt, the coyote proceeded to scrape the inside tissue away, exposing the desired layer of dick skin beneath. Bile rose in Wax's throat, but he swallowed it down, not daring to vomit in Sloan's workshop, and the opossum watched Sloan unpin the skin, roll it up, and deposit it on the table with the sewing machine.

"Easy as pie," said the coyote. "Now, let's see what you brought me."

Accepting the bag from Wax, Sloan emptied the dick onto the skinning table. It rolled to the center and Wax saw tears spring into the coyote's eyes. Sloan's chest hitched, his lips pressed together, and he snorted through his nose. Unable to restrain himself any longer, the coyote erupted into manic laughter. Sloan doubled over, clutching his stomach.

"Oh my—" Sloan gasped. "Oh—oh."

Another gale of laughter tore the breath from Sloan's lungs, and Wax eyed the stairs, preparing to flee from the crazed coyote.

"Just—" Sloan's eyes bulged. He fell to his knees. "Just look—"

The coyote's cheeks were streaked with tears as he attempted to regain control. He crawled to the worktable and dragged himself up, still seized by sporadic convulsions.

Sloan's paw shook as he poured a glass of scotch and knocked back the amber liquid. After several minutes, he wiped his eyes with his sleeve.

"It's black," Sloan said.

And, as the coyote watched the realization dawning on Wax's face, Sloan began to laugh again. "You get me, Wax? It's black, man, and it's—"

"It's not going to match," Wax said.

Sloan drew in a deep breath, composed himself, and rejoined Wax at the table. "I'll give you the good news," the coyote said. "This thing is fucking huge. It counts for two. That means you've only got two to go."

5

Huddled under a sheet between the legs of a newly deceased corpse, Wax thought that the morgue was turning out to be his worst idea yet.

The opossum had wormed his way into the coroner's office through the ventilation system, but the coroner was behind in his work and stayed after hours, until Wax's legs were numb from crouching inside a metal cabinet.

Wax had never witnessed an autopsy and couldn't understand the need to pick through a body's insides and find out what killed it—dead was dead. Therefore, when the coroner had finished removing the organs, switched off the tape recorder, and vacated the room to answer the phone, Wax assumed that the procedure had reached its end.

He sneaked across the room and shimmied up the icy metal leg of the slab. Except for the yawning crimson hole in his chest, the dead man could have been sleeping. Wax extended a paw, patted the man's stubbled cheek and pulled up an eyelid, just to be certain. Satisfied, the opossum burrowed under the white sheet that covered the man from the waist down, shuddering at the lifeless cold that emanated from the refrigerated body.

6 DICKS

The opossum groped between the corpse's legs, found the dead man's dick—growing stiff with the onset of rigor mortis—and heard the laboratory door swing open. The coroner had returned.

Wax heard the coroner switch on the tape recorder and resume his observations. The opossum resisted the urge to sneeze, as pubic hair tickled his sensitive nose. Fortunately, the dead man was overweight, and his ample belly and thighs disguised the bulge of the opossum pressed flat against the corpse's leg. Through a gap in the sheet, Wax watched the coroner close the dead man's chest cavity. Gagging, Wax waited for the coroner to pull back the sheet—to discover the live animal cowering in a nest of pubes.

A phone rang, went to voicemail. The phone rang again, and the coroner sighed, pulling the sheet to fully cover the dead man and grumbling to himself about the secretary's incompetence, as though he had forgotten it was one o'clock in the morning.

With a swish of the razor, Wax completed his task and tunneled from beneath the sheet. He removed the grate leading to the ventilation system, tossed the dick inside, and followed it, closing the vent behind him seconds before the coroner returned.

At the sight of the stain forming where the sheet concealed the dead man's genitals, the coroner dropped his clipboard and froze, eyebrows raised.

Wax felt sympathy for the man. It wasn't every day that a dick just up and vanished.

***

Sloan squinted at Wax with suspicion. The coyote said, "You mean to tell me that this went off without a hitch?"

Wax puffed out his chest and said, "Yeah. Well, mostly."

Running his tongue over his gold tooth, Sloan lit a cigarette and said, "Mostly, huh? Where'd you get it?"

"Trade secret," said Wax.

"Uh . . . huh." Sloan spun the revolver on his desk and stopped it with his paw, barrel pointed at the opossum.

Wax raised his paws. "The morgue."

"Ah," the coyote said. "Put your paws down."

Lowering his paws, Wax waited for the inevitable berating to begin.

Instead, Sloan tilted his head and said, "One to go."

6

Wax snugged the baseball cap low over his round black ears and concealed his pointed, white-furred muzzle in shadow. A cold wind ruffled the fur of his scruff, sending a shiver down his spine. Wax tucked his pink tail, numb from the evening chill, into his pants and flipped up the collar of the child-sized puffy coat he had purchased from goodwill the night before. Although Wax doubted an oncoming driver would have time to notice the tiny details of the disguise, the opossum completed the outfit with a pair of mittens and was grateful for the added warmth. Over the puffy jacket, Wax donned a reflector vest to ensure that he would be seen.

Wax stood behind the metal guardrail lining the highway, his eyes fixed on the digital numbers that flashed below the posted speed limit of thirty-five miles per hour, as the radar clocked the speed of oncoming vehicles. Beyond, a series of yellow road signs with black arrows were spaced at intervals along a sharp curve in the highway, marking the barrier between the asphalt and the steep incline that sloped to the river below. After observing the passing cars for twenty minutes—the sway of an SUV around the curve as the radar blinked "TOO FAST;" the alarming rocking of a semi-truck's trailer—Wax unfolded a bright green flyer and checked his watch.

"PARTY BUS," the flyer screamed. "XXX FURRY FRENZY!!! 2 CITIES, 2Xs THE FUN!!!" A black and white photograph showed an enthusiastic group of costumed humans with alcohol bottles held high. Below, in a smaller but equally crazed font, the flyer read: "$20 per person, 10 PM Saturday. Limited seating/ Call NOW to reserve!"

Wax had called the listed number earlier in the day, learning that the bus's seating was indeed full. The woman on the phone had provided the specifics of the two-city tour anyways, but Wax was only interested in the time of transit between cities.

The clock read 10:14 PM, when the bus drove into view. Its blaring music and colorful lights made the bus conspicuous, impossible to mistake for anything but a party-on-wheels. When the radar machine began to blink "TOO FAST," Wax stepped into the road.

6 DICKS

The bus's headlights blinded Wax, as the opossum toddled upright into the center of the lane. The bus driver—mistaking the clothed opossum for a small child—jerked the wheel and veered past Wax, close enough to blow the cap from the opossum's head. The driver over-corrected; the bus's weight shifted from the left tires to the right and started to tip. The vehicle struck the guardrail, obliterated a yellow road sign, and hung suspended for a long moment before crashing to the ground.

Wax rushed to the side of the road to watch the bus descend the incline in a death roll. The roof crushed in and the windows exploded outwards in a glittering shower of glass. Another slow-motion rotation and the tires were wrenched sideways on their axles; a strike on an outcropping of rock caved in the bus's side. The metal screamed, the inside of the bus awash with chaotic light and flying limbs. Wax caught sight of a furry spotted leg protruding from a broken window before the bus slammed down, reducing the leg to a splatter of crimson.

The bus settled at the foot of the incline, lying on its side with the rear of the vehicle submerged in the rushing river. Wax giggled, then clapped a hand over his mouth. He removed a mitten and chewed his nails, waiting.

He waited.

And listened.

The night air was cold, silent. A restless owl hooted in the distance, and three cars sped past without stopping. When no one emerged from the bus, Wax shouldered an empty backpack and followed the path of destruction downhill, stepping over broken glass and debris as he made his way to the bus's final resting place.

A single headlight sputtered, showing brief glimpses of the bus driver lying several yards from the wreckage. The driver had plunged through the shattered windshield, the furry suit slashed to ribbons and saturated with spreading crimson stains—a leopard with its head on backwards—and Wax wondered if the human head inside had twisted with the mask. The opossum rolled the leopard onto its back and searched the suit for a hidden fly. When he found the opening, he was pleased to discover that the driver was male. Wax removed the man-beast's dick and deposited it in the backpack.

Wax crawled up onto the bus's side and dropped through the

crooked door, regarding the carnage with an unexpected sense of pride. Blood painted the walls and seats, dripping onto Wax from the bent metal above and splashing under his paws, as the opossum made his way through the bus, counting fifteen humans in addition to the bus driver—all unmoving.

The furry corpses littered the floor. A rabbit drooped over a seat, the limp arms of its furry suit deformed by the snapped human limbs inside. The upper half of a wolf had tumbled through a broken window, becoming pinched underneath the bus, the lower half of the body trailing intestines tangled with party tinsel. In the water flooding the back of the bus, a seal's head bobbed with a stump of human neck jutting from the mask's hole. There were others: a fox folded backwards, nose to tail; a bear with its skull smashed by a smoke machine; a dog missing its leg. Wax winced as he squeezed past a furry cat. The costume's hindquarters reeked of human shit, and Wax was relieved when his groping hand encountered a vagina. Blood, he could handle, but the opossum couldn't stomach the thought of walking back to town with the smell of shit emanating from his backpack.

Wax frisked the bodies one by one, harvesting a total of nine dicks from the deceased passengers of the party bus. As he took a last look at the destruction, Wax rubbed at his throbbing erection and ejaculated on the upturned face of a raccoon.

***

The suit was complete.

Sloan held it up for Wax, turning the silkie this way and that, and helped the opossum into the suit. The dick skin sealed tight around his furry body, and Wax moaned as he rubbed his hands over the material, stroking and caressing. Seconds later, the opossum came hard—the intensity of the orgasm weakening his knees—and sank into Sloan's desk chair, a blissful smile stretching under the mask's skin.

"That's not all," Sloan said. His gold tooth winked. "Because you did so fucking well, there's a bonus."

The coyote held up a second suit and Wax gasped.

Sloan nodded and said, "For the ladies. So you can have your cake and eat it too."

THE OTHERS

C.M. SAUNDERS

FIRST DATES ARE WEIRD. That whole feeling out process. Did it ever occur to you that in the early stages of a relationship, both parties are just putting on a front? You are so keen to make a good impression that, subconsciously or otherwise, you modify your behaviour. Best foot forward and all that. The result is that you both end up falling in love with a false representation. A rose-tinted reflection.

And when the façade melts away is usually when most relationships start to crumble. If it even gets that far. It usually doesn't. Not for the easy come, easy go Tinder generation. We watched our parents swallow the bitter pill, work hard in jobs they hated, and slowly suffocate in loveless marriages. It just made them cold and fucking cynical. Us, we want everything here and now, baby. We'll pay for it later. Maybe.

Marilynn with two 'n's was late. I expected that. It's what girls do, right? Just to exacerbate the situation, I arrived early. I grabbed a window table and a latte, and sat in Starbucks playing with my phone for forty minutes. Did a little swiping. Okay, it was mostly swiping. But in my defence, I usually swipe left. I'm picky. Besides, if I hooked up with someone else whilst waiting for her late ass it would be Marilynn's own fault.

Eventually, she arrived. She must have spotted me through the window and recognized me from my profile picture, because she came right over: her slim, petite figure gracefully weaving through the tables, an anxious, slightly apologetic smile parting her painted red lips. "James? Sorry I'm late. Got on the wrong bus."

"No worries. It happens." I slid off my stool and stood to greet her, instinctively holding my hand out for a formal handshake.

Marilynn took it and gave it a brisk shake. Her skin felt damp, clammy to the touch. Not that it detracted from how beautiful she was. The most striking thing about her was her hair. Black, shiny and cut into a neat bob, it perfectly framed her face. Flawless skin, almond eyes, and a cute little upturned nose completed the image.

I told her to take a seat and left her guarding the table while I went to the counter to grab her a coffee and a refill for myself. She asked for filter. With six sachets of brown sugar. Six. Obviously, I dropped a lame line about her being sweet enough without all that sugar. But she just me gave a tired smile, as if she'd heard it a hundred times before.

When I came back, I found her sitting with her back to the wall, looking around skittishly. I completely understood. I was anxious as hell, and I was a grown man. I can only imagine how much more vulnerable women must feel, when every time they go out, they risk another #metoo moment. It wasn't like we'd been chatting a long time. Only a few days. But we hit it off, and it just so happened that we were both heading to town the same day. It was like fate.

She looked a little relieved to see me, and I immediately tried to put her at ease by keeping it light and talking about the usual, random shit: the weather, Love Island, Ed Sheeran's new single which we both agreed wasn't quite as good as the last but would probably still sell two million copies. After a while Marilynn thawed, and began opening up a little. We moved on to her second cup of coffee and my third while we talked about our favourite holiday destinations, our friends, and our hopes for the future. Only when I asked whether she'd a happy childhood did a shadow cross her face.

The question seemed innocuous enough, but its effect was extraordinary. She stammered, opened her mouth to say something, then had a change of heart and closed it again. You can probably imagine the kinds of things running through my head: a broken home, divorced parents, an alcoholic stepdad, schoolyard bullying, some awful childhood illness, the death of a sibling, some form of abuse.

Sensing I might have just inadvertently hobbled myself I apologised and, in an effort to get things back on track, asked her what her favourite book was. Weak, I know, but I was really struggling with my game by this point. The day had started so promisingly and now I could feel it all slipping away.

Marilynn was unimpressed. From that point on our conversation was stilted and awkward, a fact reflected in her body language, which became increasingly guarded. Before long she was sitting ramrod straight with her arms folded. She may as well have been holding up a big sign saying GET THE FUCK AWAY FROM ME.

It was all one-way traffic, and pretty soon I decided to cut my losses. I drained the dregs in my coffee mug, thanked Marilynn for her time, and stood up.

"Don't leave," she said.

I paused in the act of putting on my coat, confusion creasing my brow. "Why?"

"Because I don't want to be alone."

I sat back down, one arm in my coat and one arm out. Normally I would think she was just some chick yanking my chain, but something about her demeanour persuaded me otherwise. She bowed her head and looked up at me, those big almond eyes flickering with the merest hint of desperation.

I should have walked out anyway. I should have left that Starbucks and never looked back. But you know what they say about hindsight being a wonderful thing.

As it happened, I sat back in my chair.

"I suppose I owe you an explanation," Marilynn said, her voice faltering.

"There's no need." I wanted to know. Of course I did. But at the same time, I didn't want to make things even weirder than they already were. Looking back, I firmly believe there was something else at play, too. Call it instinct or intuition, but on some level, I knew that this was a turning point. There could be no going back. You can't *unknow* something, and sometimes ignorance really is bliss.

"You're going to think I'm crazy," Marilynn said, looking around anxiously as if expecting to find someone watching her. Us.

"Sounds good," I said, offering an enthusiastic grin by way of encouragement.

"Thing is, as crazy as it sounds, this is part of me. I had a good time today, and I want to be open and honest with you. If this . . . thing . . . is a deal breaker, you never have to see me again."

"Oh come on, whatever it is can't be that bad. I dated a girl who had chronic flatulence before." That raised a small but genuine smile. "So, come on. Spit it out."

"Okay, well . . . " Marilynn paused to gather herself. "I see . . . stuff."

"What kind of stuff? Dead people?" I said, referencing the famous line from Sixth Sense. I was hoping to lighten the mood, but my attempt fell flat. I keep forgetting not everyone is a connoisseur of cheesy nineties horror flicks.

"If only it was that simple."

"Then what do you see?"

"Others."

"Other what?"

"Other things."

"What kind of things?" This conversation was going nowhere fast.

"Aardvarks, mostly. Those animals with big long snouts? To eat ants? They walk around on two legs, like people, wearing clothes and chatting to each other. Except they're bigger than I imagined them to be. Wild ones, I mean."

That was unexpected. I laughed so hard it was more of an uncultured guffaw. Someone on the next table gave me a disapproving look and my hand instinctively went to cover my mouth and nose in case any unsightly snot came out. That wouldn't be a good look. This girl had a sense of humour!

But wait—Marilynn wasn't laughing. Instead, she just sat there, arms still folded, eyes cast down. I knew that look well. It was a look of abject disappointment.

Suddenly feeling very insensitive, along with confused, I sought clarification. "You're not joking?"

Marilynn shifted nervously in her seat. "Why would I joke about that?"

For one of the few times in my life, I was truly lost for words. After an uneasy silence that stretched for perhaps half a minute, though seemed much longer, I gently prodded her. "Do you see anything else? Apart from giant aardvarks walking around wearing clothes?"

Marilynn looked up and planted her elbows on the table, leaning forward in her chair, as if she were about to tell me a secret. "Yeah. I also see a lot of huge rabbits with top hats, and brown bears, seven or eight feet tall, wearing tuxedos or suits, as if dressed up for some important social event. Sometimes I see them wearing pretty dresses, yellow or blue, but not so much. I watched one juggling coloured balls once. Faster and faster he went, until the colours were nothing but a blur. He never dropped one! Another time, I saw a civet cat. Think it was a civet cat. With the big, round eyes? This one was bigger, though. Like, as big as me. He was wearing clothes, too. Or she. It's hard to tell. I mean, I guess what sex they are by the clothes they wear, but I'm not sure if I'm just being presumptuous. You know, they could be gay."

"Could be," I volunteered.

"I didn't like the look of the civet cat, to be honest. He looked kinda . . . edgy? And sneaky. Like he would rip your face off as soon as look at you. I see a lot of normal cats, too. Mostly ginger ones, isn't that strange? I mean, I know it's not the same cat I see over and over again because I see them in groups sometimes. But they are almost always ginger. And a little overweight, if I'm honest."

"Wearing people clothes and walking on two legs?"

"Well, obviously. I mean, I know a normal cat when I see one."

"And these aren't normal cats?"

"Do they sound like normal cats?"

"Fuck no."

"Then there's your answer."

Her words were washing over me like water. I couldn't grasp them all and derive their meaning. I was snatching for them, but they were coming too fast. I needed time to digest all this. Looking back, I think I may have been lapsing into a kind of mild shock. Everything took on a surreal quality, and I began to wonder if I was dreaming.

"Are you okay?" I heard Marilynn ask. "You've gone a bit pale."

"I'm fine," I lied. "Must be all the caffeine."

"I hope I'm not freaking you out."

"Of course not. I've heard freakier," I said, even though I really hadn't. I'd heard more disgusting. Like the time Billy Lehman saw some guy fall and hit his face on a metal fence. When he got up, his eyeball was hanging halfway down his cheek. So more disgusting, yeah. But straight up freaky? No. This was on another level.

I was still hoping she was playing some kind of practical joke on me. Seeing how far she could push it. But as the minutes ticked by, that scenario became more and more unlikely. With that idea debunked, it left only two other alternatives. Either she was delusional, like shit-bag crazy, and probably dangerous with it, or she was telling the truth.

Despite a growing sense of unease, I had to know more. Some hidden, dark part of me demanded answers. "Where do they get their clothes?" I asked. "Do they have special shops selling oversized animal clothes, or do they use Amazon like everyone else?

Marilynn looked me dead in the eye and blinked once. Twice. Then said, "The fuck should I know?"

"And where do they live? Do they have little houses? Communities?"

"I think you're missing the point," Marilynn sighed.

"So, what is the point?"

"The point is, I can see these . . . things. Everywhere. And I know other people can't. Can you?"

"No."

"Look," she nodded her head toward the street outside. "Do you see that massive penguin walking past wearing a sombrero and carrying a cane?"

I looked. Of course I looked. Even craned my neck to look both up the street and down in case I'd missed it. All I saw was the usual random assortment of people scurrying past. "No, I don't see it."

"You know what I think?"

"What?"

"I think we can all see this shit when we are kids. Animals, too. I often see babies laughing and pointing at the Others. The parents just ignore them. Think they're playing."

"Is that what you call them? The Others?"

"Yep. I think as we grow up, we lose whatever ability we had to see them, and they fade away. They're still there, of course. Babies and animals can see them. But they become invisible to us and we forget our childhood experiences. You know when you're a kid everything seems normal?"

"Yeah."

"The thing with me is, I never lost the ability. I still see them. Maybe there are other people who still see them, too. I think there must be. I can't be the only one ever. But if they talked about it openly, they would sound so crazy they'd probably get institutionalized, so they keep it to themselves. Do you know what a furry is?"

"People who dress up as animals for fun?"

"Yeah. Well, sometimes I think that's an extension of it. Or related somehow. I don't know. I don't have all the answers."

"Did you tell your parents about the . . . Others?"

"Of course. Lots of times. They called them my 'imaginary friends.' Right then, I realized they couldn't see what I could see. It was hard to talk about after that, so I hid it for years. But I hope that by telling people about it now, people like you, I might find someone else who can see them. I don't even care if they lock me up in a nuthouse, because I get the feeling that's where I'm most likely to find other people like me."

"So . . . are these things from another dimension or something?"

"Who knows?"

"Do you talk to them?"

"I have done. Before."

"What, in English?"

"No. In fucking Ukrainian. What do you think?"

"Sorry, I was—"

"Sorry nothing. If you don't believe me, fine. I get it. There's no need to be facetious."

"I wasn't being fac . . . whatever you said. I'm genuinely interested."

"I bet you are."

"So, what did you talk about?"

"The weather, mostly."

"Very British."

"Indeed. I mean, what else are we going to talk about? Most of them are strangers to me. You wouldn't just walk up to some random person in the street and start talking to them about personal shit, would you?"

"Guess not."

"You know what's weird? Most of the Others don't even pay us grown-ups much attention. They just go about their business, and we go about ours. I guess they take it for granted they can't be seen, or maybe they just like being invisible. Sometimes I think . . . "

"What?"

Marilynn suddenly looked embarrassed, as if until now she had been saying perfectly normal things. "Sometimes I think they can shapeshift?"

"They can what?"

"Shapeshift. You know, make themselves look like anything they want. Maybe it's about my perception."

"I'm not following."

"Well, maybe the Others appear as these weird animals with human traits to me. That is just how I perceive them. But another person might notice them and see something completely different. That's when I look at aliens, ghosts, shadow people, demons, fairies and all this other supernatural stuff, and think it might all be the same phenomena. Or at least connected. So, do you believe in any of those things?"

"I dunno," I replied. "Aliens, maybe? It's pretty naïve, and spectacularly arrogant, to think that the only intelligent life in the whole infinite vastness of space lives here on this little floating rock."

"Very true. So, if my theory is correct, if you believe in one aspect, you believe in them all."

"Then how come I don't see massive penguins walking down the street wearing sombreros?"

"Because you're not looking. And even if you were, maybe you would see four-foot grey aliens in flying saucers instead."

God help me, by now everything Marilynn was saying had a ring of truth about it. Maybe it was her sincerity, and the conviction with which she was talking. Whether all this was real or not, she obviously believed it was and that made it real to her at least. "Most of them."

"What?" she asked, raising an eyebrow.

"You said most of them are strangers to you."

"So?"

"Well, what about the ones which aren't strangers?"

Something flickered in Marilynn's eyes and she glanced away self-consciously. "What about them?"

"Have you ever really got to know any of the Others?"

"I have."

"So tell me about it."

"What do you wanna know?" For the first time, Marilynn's tone was defensive.

"Dunno," I stammered. What *did* I want to know? "I guess, are they . . . dangerous?"

"Are people dangerous?"

"Some?"

"Well, it's the same with the Others. They all have different personalities and are all separate entities. Some are good; some are bad. Very bad."

"What have you seen them do?"

"Well, there's Bad Panda who gets . . . "

"Gets what?"

"Forget it. I shouldn't tell you. Anyway, this has been fun. I should get going now. Maybe we can do it again. If I haven't weirded you out too much, that is." She suddenly got to her feet and looked around nervously, as if checking the coast was clear, before her eyes settled on the exit.

I couldn't let her go. Not like this. It felt like she'd been telling a very long joke and was about to leave before delivering the punch line. "You've told me this much." I protested. "And I'm still here. I think I deserve to know the full story."

Marilynn paused and looked me up and down "Are you sure?"

"Yes." Except suddenly, I wasn't. I wasn't sure at all.

"Might as well get this over with now, this way we don't waste any more dates if you think I'm . . . " She took a breath. "Bad Panda is, well, a panda. But bigger. Much bigger. Not that I've ever seen any other pandas, but I doubt they'd be eight or nine feet tall like him. He sometimes wears sunglasses. Which is funny. He wears ones with bright red frames. If he didn't, you wouldn't even know he was even wearing sunglasses because of the black around his eyes," she chuckled coquettishly, covering her mouth with a delicate hand. "He's so cute sometimes."

"If he's so cute, why do you call him Bad Panda?"

"I've been seeing him ever since I was a little girl. He's one of the few I can talk to. We always understood each other. Not just in a language way, but in every way. He's my friend. Like you would call your cat or dog your friend." She seemed not to have heard my question. I was about to ask it again, when her face darkened. "The thing is, he gets jealous. Hates it when I spend time with anyone else. He can't always process his emotions, so then he lashes out."

"And he gives you a hard time?"

"No . . . but it does make dating sort of hard." She sighed; clearly this was why she'd seemed so distant all night. "He doesn't want to hurt me. He loves me. He'd never hurt me physically. He just gets angry at other people easily. When he gets really angry, he can sometimes cross over and affect this world. It's the strangest thing. Rare, I suppose. I always took it as a sign of how deeply he cares about me."

"Affect this world how?"

"When I was little, this kid down the block, Michelle, she used to pick on me. One day she tried to make me eat worms. It was terrible. Then she took off on her bike, but . . . she fell. Well, he *pushed* Michelle off her bike. I know he did. I saw him do it through my tears. She didn't pick on me anymore at least. He was even more possessive when I played with boys. There was a boy in my street called Timothy. He was a nice enough boy, but when I started to see him every day—well, one day, bad Panda picked him up and threw him against a wall. Hurt his back really bad. After that, I didn't play with Timothy anymore. You know, to protect him. That's what Bad Panda wanted, I suppose. Timothy said later it felt like a gust of wind had blown him over. But I think he knew I was responsible somehow. I could tell by the way he looked at me. I'll never forget that look of fear."

"So, he protects you?"

"Mostly. It gets worse. I got filthy drunk one night in my Freshman year at college and this guy I liked took me home. We woke up in the middle of the night, after we'd had sex, and the bed was shaking. Violently shaking. This guy couldn't see Bad Panda, of course, but I could. I've never seen anyone run as fast as that in my life. Needless to say, he never came over again. Then there was Adam, my first real boyfriend."

"What happened to him?"

"Never mind. You seem like a real nice guy and *if* you want to go out again, I figured you should at least know how protective and jealous Bad Panda can be. It's something we both have to take into consideration"

"Marilynn?"

"Yeah?"

"Does Bad Panda know you're here with me?"

"Well, he kinda knows where I am most of the time. Follows me around, see. Like a big cuddly stalker. I saw him standing in the far corner for a while." Marilynn nodded at some space behind me. I turned to look, but of course saw nothing out of the ordinary. "He's gone now," Marilynn clarified. "I think he just came to check on me. He was trying to blend in, bless him. As if a giant panda with red-framed sunglasses could blend in anywhere, ha-ha!"

I tried to join in the laughter, but all that came out was a strangled murmur. There was a sinking feeling in my stomach. "Marilynn, I didn't tease you or anything, right? I mean, will Bad Panda come after me?"

"Not sure. You don't even believe me anyway, do you?"

"I never said I didn't believe you, I . . . " I let the words trail off, unsure of how to finish the sentence.

"Look, I told you everything, so call me if you wanna have another date. Just keep what I told you in mind. And I meant what I said. You seem like a real nice guy. I just hope you really are . . . for your sake."

And then, Marilynn really did leave. I watched her waltz out of the Starbucks, swaying her hips and flicking her hair as she went. She didn't look back. Seconds later, I saw her pass by the window, and I swear to God she was looking up at something and smiling broadly. Something I couldn't see.

Randall Rabbit

Elliot Arthur Cross

ALL FRED WANTED WAS some cheap-ass beer so he could celebrate the passing of another year, but since his fake ID got shredded, he had to be creative. At least turning twenty meant he'd only have to wait a year until he could turn tricks for cash like an adult.

He finished a cigarette on the curb in front of the gas station while he waited. It was well past dark already and he tightened his hoodie to keep the chill from soaking in. Finally, he spotted the blue mini-van pull into the lot and ease around the side. Fred hopped up, slung his backpack over his shoulder, and stomped out his cigarette.

He jogged to the meeting place—the mini-van parked under a broken streetlight next to the dumpster—and jumped in the passenger seat, inhaling fresh pine, and enjoying the warmth from the outside world. The middle-aged woman—pretty enough but always tired-looking—in the driver's seat rummaged through a clunky purse. He'd known her a few months but never got her name. He thought of her as Mrs. Frankenstein, for her the gray streaks in her black, curly hair.

"Sorry I'm running late, it's just I—" she paused and snickered at herself, as if realizing Fred didn't deserve any canned excuse. She found her prize in her purse and looked up for the first time. "How long's it been since you came?"

"Three days," Fred said. It had really been two since someone's obese grandpa blew him for fifty bucks, but Mrs. Frankenstein was paying for the illusion more than reality.

"Right." Clearly, she didn't believe him.

"Look, I got a nice batch of boy-batter ready to go."

"Good." She pulled out a small pair of blue boxer briefs and a resealable plastic zipper bag. "I want you to put these on and soak them really good then put them in this."

"Sure." Fred took the underwear and realized while they were clean, they weren't new. Mrs. Frankenstein must have snatched them from someone, and Fred had a feeling they'd never be returned.

"I'll be back with your beer in, what five minutes?"

"Cool."

Mrs. Frankenstein left Fred alone in the mini-van. He kicked off his sneakers and shimmied out of his torn jeans and boxers as he climbed into the spacious back. He bumped the soccer ball on the floor that she'd ordered him to lick a few weeks back.

Fred managed to slide the boxer briefs up over his ass and cock. They were tighter than he liked, so he settled for squeezing himself through the cotton. He clenched his eyes shut and focused on the cock at hand. He'd never been great with his imagination. Survival instincts had never allowed him to fully lose himself in fantasies, lest he leave his body defenseless. Still, he tried to imagine feeling a tight, wet, and, most importantly, warm, pussy.

The tight underwear got more uncomfortable as he stroked himself to his full length and girth, but he was already leaking pre-cum into the fabric, proud that he was following his customer's orders.

He wondered how much time he had until Mrs. Frankenstein would return. If he wasn't done, he'd ask her to give him a hand. That would certainly help. He thought of her fingers sliding along the briefs instead of his own and promptly felt his balls tighten and his toes spasm.

It was far from his most pleasurable orgasm, but it had been two days and felt wonderful as his caged cock came. His entire crotch was soon covered in a sticky warm mess. After catching his breath, Fred peeled off the boxer briefs, leaving a gooey trail down his leg hair, and sealed them in the plastic baggie.

He was dressed and tying his second shoe when Mrs. Frankenstein returned with two six-packs. He tossed them in his backpack and she hurried him out of the mini-van like an unwanted houseguest. Back in the cold again, Fred braced himself from a gust of wind, and hurried out of the parking lot toward his shithole apartment.

When he slipped inside and closed the door, he locked it, and slid the chain into place. Safe at last. Or at least safe against anyone with weak shoulders.

Fred kicked off his shoes and carried his backpack to the kitchen. He set both six-packs in the basically empty fridge but kept one can out for himself. He cracked it open and took a refreshing gulp. He hoped Mrs. Frankenstein was enjoying the still drying briefs while he drank. It would be nice if there was one person out there with him on her mind, even if she didn't care about him.

He plopped into the uneven kitchen chair and drummed his fingers on the table. He'd turn twenty tomorrow, in just a few hours really, and he couldn't think of a thing to do besides sit at home and drink and smoke alone.

He supposed it was his own damn fault he didn't have anyone around to celebrate with. It wasn't like he'd always made the best choices.

As Fred mused on his abundance of shortcomings, he shuffled into his room for a pack of smokes. He lit up, thankful for the distraction.

A little late-night company was exactly what he needed. Anything to stave off the loneliness, especially tonight.

He looked through his contacts listlessly until a new message notification appeared.

NEWUSERID8U: Hello, boy. Are you lonely tonight?

FREDDY_VERSBIBOY: howd u know?

NEWUSERID8U: Gut instinct. I'd like to keep you company tonight.

FREDDY_VERSBIBOY: yay. gimme 20 mins 2 get clean 4 u.

Fred gave the john his address and finished his cigarette, then took a scalding shower, rubbing his flesh pink.

Fred dried off and slipped into a pair of jeans and a tank top, not bothering with underwear. He strode to the kitchen, grabbed a beer, and took a sip just as someone started knocking on his apartment door.

Good timing.

Fred opened the door and a cold shiver ran through his shoulders and down his spine, erupting in a wave of nausea in his gut.

Randall Rabbit.

A man in a rabbit fursuit stood in the hallway, the black eyes staring down at him. Fred dropped his drink, the can clunking against one foot, spilling foamy beer onto the floor. It soaked the carpet like a rentboy shooting into skimpy boxer briefs.

Why did it have to be a goddamn rabbit of all things? Sure, the fursuit looked similar to Randall Rabbit, but it wasn't identical. He was a skinny figure with a large head, wearing gloves and a stained pair of sweatpants.

The fur didn't move. Fred stepped back from the spilt beer and picked it up.

"Sorry, just surprised. Um, come on in, you wascally wabbit."

The fur strode in and closed the door behind him.

He's not Randall Rabbit . . .

"You want a drink?" Fred asked.

The fur shook his head no.

"Mind if I drink?"

Another identical headshake, so Fred wiped dirt off the beer and took a sip.

The fur sat on the couch and patted his lap twice. Fred nodded and sat where he was instructed. The fur rubbed his neck and shoulders, then Fred's stomach. His big, clumsy fingers pawed at Fred's crotch and began tugging on his jeans.

"You're eager, huh?" Fred purred. The john nodded.

Fred finished his beer and stood. He made a show of unzipping his jeans and sliding them down to the floor.

Before he knew it, the fur was up in a flash and bending Fred over the arm of the couch.

While the fur started grunting and fucking him, all Fred could do was think about a stupid stuffed animal that he hadn't seen since he turned seventeen.

***

Fred hated his stupid foster brother's fucking stuffed animal. Glenn had it wherever he went whenever he was home. He'd enter the house, scamper off to wherever he'd hidden it, and carry it around until it was time to leave the house again. That's when he'd squirrel the damn thing away. Glenn called it Randall Rabbit and insisted it sit on the table when he ate and sat on his lap when he watched TV.

The Pecks were an older couple who'd been fostering teens for the last thirty years. Mr. Peck was retired, losing his hearing, and spent most of his day in the reclining chair in front of the TV, screaming at old detective movies. Mrs. Peck was a lunch lady who didn't take any back talk. Of all his foster parents, they were easily the best. They only ever had two kids at a time, and they didn't care too much or too little. Friendly enough, and without *Full House* emotional speeches.

Fred figured he had it easy with them. He'd sail onto eighteen and maybe even keep in touch with them after moving out. But then the pipsqueak moved in and they started doting on him, and he carried that fucking stuffed toy *everywhere*. The kid would freak out if anyone even touched it, and he'd shove it in their faces.

On the night Fred turned seventeen, giving himself exactly one more year to enjoy suckling Uncle Sam's teat, he went out partying with a few delinquent friends. It was a sad affair, but he'd managed to get good and buzzed off stolen wine coolers.

Fred returned to the house after the Pecks had gone to bed. Fred was horny and frustrated, having been shot down for a birthday blowjob from a slutty college girl who gave his friend a handjob. He stumbled into the room he shared with Glenn, who was reading a comic book with the rabbit.

Glenn got up, Randall Rabbit in hand, and Fred stopped him. "Where you going, twerp?"

"Bathroom."

"You need that stuffed toy to go in there with you?" Fred asked. "Your bunny into piss play?"

"Shut up!"

"Relax, idiot," Fred said. "Just leave the rabbit here. Don't be a weirdo."

"All right." Glenn frowned, but left the room just the same.

Glenn needed to grow up. What better way than to force him to stop dragging that filthy thing around and shoving it in everyone's faces?

In a year, Fred would be out on his ass, and that twerp Glenn would still be trotting around the Pecks' house, carrying that filthy stuffed animal. It wasn't right. Fred seized the rabbit and squeezed it, grunting into its cold black eyes.

He couldn't wait for the little fucker to tear open so they could trash the thing.

Maybe he wouldn't have to wait. Maybe Fred deserved to give himself a birthday gift.

Drunk and horny, and filled with jealousy, Fred pulled out his switchblade and stabbed into the Rabbit's ass, ripping open a suitable hole under the floppy tail, exposing the pure white stuffing inside.

Fred dropped the knife and whipped out his dick. All of his hatred and jealousy coursed through his bloodstream, plumping up his manhood. He thrust himself into the hole and proceeded to fuck Randall Rabbit. He could feel himself leaking precum, soaking the stuffing as it stuck to his slick stick.

The bedroom door creaked open and Glenn stood in the threshold. His jaw went wide, and he gasped. He ran toward Fred crying, but Fred shoved him back with one hand.

"Please!" Glenn begged. "He's my only friend! He's all I have! Please!" He was racked with sobs. "You're killing him!"

"Nah, he's begging for it. What a slutty bunny."

"Please, please, please, oh god, please."

"This is good," Fred moaned to Glenn. "Now I get why you're always carrying this fucker around."

Fred thrust his hips violently while he slid the rabbit back and forth, long dicking it. It felt incredible. All of his anxieties and frustrations were building up in his gut and he twisted the stuffed toy, wringing its neck.

"Please don't kill him." Glenn was rocking back and forth. He stuck his thumb in his mouth, tears streaming from his eyes.

Fred couldn't believe the meltdown he was causing. The kid needed this. He had to toughen up or he'd never make it. He buried himself to his balls in the moist stuffing, tearing through the virginal territory deeper toward the head. He could feel his orgasm building, but he held off, relishing the moment, eager for it to last. His life was shit, so he could at least take pleasure in the small things.

Fred gripped the head, his biceps bulging, and tore through the mouth with his cock.

"Look, Randall Rabbit is sticking his tongue out." Fred laughed, swiveling his hips back and forth.

That was too much for Fred. He pulled back, keeping his dick in the rabbit's guts and came. Glenn was on the floor, practically hyperventilating.

Once Fred caught his breath, he peeled off the wet stuffed animal and dropped it to the floor with a plop.

"I don't think he made it," Fred snickered. "You know what that means? Viking funeral."

He grabbed his lighter from his desk and promptly set Randall Rabbit on fire. Fred watched, laughing, as the stuffed animal burned. He turned to Glenn and his smile dropped. The kid's eyes were wide and unblinking, his face completely expressionless.

"Hey, snap out of it." Fred feigned a punch, but the kid didn't flinch.

Shit, he broke him. He knew Glenn would be upset, but come on. He just needed to sleep it off. They both did.

Fred disposed of the rabbit's remains and put Glenn to bed. The kid didn't move a muscle, aside from a slow, steady breathing. Fred went to bed and woke up, only to find Glenn still unresponsive.

"Wake the fuck up," Fred hissed, shaking him. Nothing.

That's when he told the Pecks. They freaked out and rushed Glenn to the hospital, leaving Fred alone in the house.

After Glenn was declared catatonic and checked into a mental facility full time, Child Services investigated. All the time, Fred waited for the noose to tighten, but no one ever blamed him. There were suspicious looks, certainly, but that was it.

While Fred helped Mrs. Peck pack Glenn's things, he couldn't help but feel guilty while she looked for Randall Rabbit.

"No idea where the thing could be?" she asked in a huff.

"No. I'll get him a new stuffed animal."

"That's nice, but I doubt it'll help. That rabbit was special."

"How?" Fred asked, although he really didn't want to know.

RANDALL RABBIT

"Glenn's family all died in a fire six years ago. They found him a block away, cradling the rabbit, claiming Randall saved him. It's the only thing he cared about keeping from each foster family. Maybe he'll snap out of it if we find it?"

"Yeah, maybe." Fred couldn't wait to turn eighteen and leave the house so he wouldn't ever have to think about what he'd done again.

***

Fred lost all track of time as he spaced out and got ready for the john to give him a rough fucking on the couch. It was nice to get out of his head and have the company, even if it was shallow and would leave him feeling empty come sunrise.

He felt the cotton of the john's glove part his lips and slide inside. He suckled and chewed, playing his role as an obedient sub. As he did, the moistened glove loosened and came off between his teeth. He expected the familiar taste of salty flesh, but Fred felt a thick wad of hair invade his mouth. Had the john been wearing gloves over fur mittens? His hands hadn't looked that bulky, but as Fred was rocked back and forth, he had to admire the dedication.

He also had to cringe at all the wet hair in his mouth.

Just then, the john leaned over him, pressing his warm body against Fred's back, and sticking a rough, wet tongue in his ear.

It wasn't altogether unpleasant, although it was surprising. It also didn't feel like a normal tongue. It ran up and down the back of his head, probing inside his ear, in and out, along the base of his skull. It was long, and it was all wrong.

He just needed to figure it out. He chewed lightly on the hairy fingers in his mouth, but they didn't give way like they should. They were firm, and he could feel the hard edges of the fingers. There was no give and take of gloves over fingers, they felt like real fingers. It was a real tongue . . .

He's not human!

Fred tried to scream, but the furry digits forced themselves down his throat, spreading his lips, gagging him. He struggled for breath, saliva spilling down his chin.

When the fingers retracted from his mouth, Fred drew quick breath, eager to expand his lungs. The relief was short-lived, as the john went to work on Fred's ass.

At first, it was a not too unpleasant burn as his ass stretched wider to accommodate those slick fingers.

Weak and scrunched against his rough couch, Fred tried tilting his head back, wimpering for the rabbit monster to leave. He felt furry fingers on both hands inside him, spreading him wide. His ass stretched further than ever before, the burn was deeper than ever before. Fred cried as something inside his anus tore. Warm blood fell on his ankles, his ass numb from pain.

The rabbit positioned his hips behind Fred's ruined asshole and started feeding it his freakishly massive member.

The rabbit's hands were vices on Fred's narrow hips as he grew and grew inside him. Fred's body went cold and sweat covered his face and back. He could barely make sense of it as the rabbit's member burrowed deeper and deeper, like some unending cock.

Fred opened one eye against the arm of the couch and craned his neck so he could look down his torso to his stomach. The outline of the rabbit's prick was approaching his navel.

Fred brought his hand against his bulging abdomen and felt his skin stretch as the giant prick forced itself deeper inside him, shredding his insides.

It passed through his belly button, and suddenly, the breath caught in Fred's chest in a white-hot flash of pain. His lungs could no longer fully inflate, they were pressed against the intruder.

The rabbit's prick tore finally through Fred's throat. His gaze dropped to the tip as it poked out from under his chin.

As Fred's life slipped away, all he could think was that it looked like he was sticking out his tongue.

A Concubine for the Hive

RUE K. POE

LORA RIPPED A WEED from the loose soil of her herb garden, enjoying the sound of its roots tearing apart. She dropped it into a basket and looked at her husband. Randy weeded next to her, a dumb grin on his face. Perspiration beaded on his pink forehead, shadowed beneath the visor of a baseball cap. He looked like he was having fun.

She grabbed another stalk and yanked. She missed flowers.

"Lora! That was *rosemary*." Randy made an exasperated motion with his hand as he scolded her.

"How am I supposed to tell the difference? They all look the same."

"If you don't know, you ought to ask before pulling it. Let me have that rosemary, we can use it."

She passed him the herb. Both of their hands were filthy. Lora frowned at the dirt caked under her nails. She didn't see the point in getting this dirty for herbs. How much damn rosemary could two people eat, anyway? Bored with the project, she looked around the backyard. Their owl box, an oversized wooden birdhouse, lay broken beneath a tree.

"When did the birdhouse fall?" she asked.

Randy scoffed. "Weeks ago. I reckon you wouldn't have noticed. You ain't tended this garden worth a damn, Lora."

"I wanted a flower garden, not an herb garden."

Randy glared at her but said nothing. He'd already fought and won this battle. A flower garden would have attracted too many pollinators, and Randy's bee allergy was too severe to take any risks. An herb garden was the logical compromise, he'd said.

Lora sighed and half-heartedly pulled another weed.

She looked at Randy's belly hanging over the waistband of his jeans. When had he gotten so fat? She tore apart the weed she'd just pulled, thinking about the men she used to bed. Beautiful, virile men with strong arms and foreign tongues. Lora reckoned she'd do anything for one more night of passion, of heavy breathing and spilled wine.

"I need to run to the store," she said.

"Are you serious? We said we'd do this today."

"I'm gonna get some weed killer so we don't have to worry about it anymore."

Randy pinched the bridge of his nose. "I already told you, we can't use weed killer. That would kill the herbs."

"Maybe they have weed killer that's safe for herb gardens. It can't hurt to look."

Randy returned to the weeds, looking defeated.

The hardware store was a quick trip into town. Lora listened to an 80's station on the ten-minute drive—a nice change of pace from Randy's country playlist. Being free of Randy energized her, like a chest full of fresh air. She hummed as their small Tennessee town buzzed by. She even rolled the window down to let her red hair catch the wind.

She saw the flowers as soon as she pulled into the parking lot, their bright colors calling to her from the Lawn & Garden section. She exited the vehicle and hurried over, eager to touch their petals.

There were pansies in every shade of the rainbow, each bloom a welcoming face. Delicate, fleeting pops of summer, bursts of life that would be dead by Christmas. Flowers were pretty to look at and never overstayed their welcome. Lora appreciated that. She lowered her face into one and breathed its sweet perfume. She imagined the house and backyard sitting empty, waiting for her. She'd fill it all with flowers, make it look like a fairytale. Her suitors would come and go, never staying long enough to bitch and moan, to gain weight. In her daydream, Randy had simply ceased to exist.

A piercing cry jerked Lora out of her fantasy. She looked behind her and grimaced at the crying baby, wriggling and pink with rage.

Its young mother soothed it, but her efforts only made it worse. Another scream snaked down Lora's spine. She wanted to pinch its little nose shut and press her palm against its slimy mouth. Thank Christ Randy couldn't have children.

Something in her peripheral vision grabbed her attention. A bright yellow cardboard display stood adjacent to the pansies, its gaudy color demanding to be noticed. At its top, a cartoon bee with a toothy smile held a flower out to her. Bold green letters read:

Dr. B's Honeybee Attractant
Bring the swarm to you!

Lora had never heard of such a thing as honeybee attractant, but she was drawn to the display like a moth to a flame. The cardboard shelves held neat rows of small yellow boxes, and she plucked one carefully. The box felt surprisingly lightweight in her hand. She shook it lightly, the contents sliding around. A wicked idea began to form.

"That stuff works," came a deep voice behind her.

Lora jumped in surprise, then turned to face the source of the interruption. A square-jawed, teenage boy stood before her, wearing the navy-blue vest that identified him as an employee.

"Does it, now?" she asked, noticing the biceps poking out of his sleeves.

"Yes, ma'am. We use it on my dad's farm. Attracts a lot of bees."

"How does it work?" Lora spoke to the boy's nipples, hard beneath his damp t-shirt.

"Well, I couldn't tell you the science behind it, but you just leave some in a bait hive and wait a couple weeks. That's all there is to it."

"A bait hive," Lora repeated. She didn't know why she said it out loud. The words felt good on her tongue.

She paid cash for the honeybee attractant and left the box in a garbage can at the shop door. All that remained was a little plastic vial full of amber-colored liquid. She stuck it in her pocket and tried to act natural on her walk back to the car. She kept the radio turned off on the drive home. Her mind was racing. Did she dare?

Randy was inside when she got home, watching a baseball game on TV.

"You get that weed killer?" he asked.

"Huh?"

"The weed killer safe for herb gardens," he said in a condescending tone.

"Oh. No," Lora said. "They didn't have any."

He grunted as if to say, 'I told you so.'

Lora walked out to the backyard and looked it over, searching for a place to leave the bait. Her eyes fell on the owl box. She smirked and wondered how long it would be until Randy got around to fixing it. A couple of weeks, at least. Lora walked over and gave it a good kick, just in case anything was holed up inside. When nothing came scurrying out, she lifted the hinged lid. The inside was empty save for a few dead bugs and abandoned cobwebs, and she shook them out before setting it back in place. She pulled the vial out of her pocket and cracked it open.

She'd forgotten to read the instructions before tossing them. Shrugging, she dumped the entire contents of the vial into the wooden box. She closed the lid and examined the birdhouse. As far as she could tell, it didn't look tampered with. Satisfied, she snuck over to the neighbor's backyard and dropped the empty vial in their trash can. There was nothing left to do but wait.

***

Lora began each morning with a mental countdown. She started at one, and day by day counted up to fourteen. Two weeks, just long enough for the bait hive to lure a small swarm. The owl box remained where it fell, wide circular entrance gaping open like a hungry mouth, wood bleaching in the sun.

On the fourteenth day, Lora woke up early. Anxious and giddy, she snuck out of bed and crept outside to check on the bait hive.

That snake oil probably doesn't work anyway, she thought as she walked. She was almost to the birdhouse when her stomach dropped down to her knees and her blood ran cold. The unmistakable buzzing came from within the box. With movements as quiet and careful as a cat she knelt beside the birdhouse and lowered her ear to the wood. A deep hum thrummed from inside. The sound of a busy swarm. Her mouth fell open.

Lora's heart raced as she hurried back inside. Waiting for Randy to wake up was torture, but she busied herself for a couple of hours until the sounds of his stirring came from the bedroom. She put on a pot of coffee and collected herself, needing everything that followed to seem natural. After dragging himself out of bed and taking a piss, Randy appeared in the kitchen to drink his morning coffee. As Lora spoke, she made a conscious effort to keep her voice steady.

"I reckon we ought to fix that birdhouse today. Wanna help me?" she said.

Randy shrugged and nodded from behind his mug.

"Let's get it done, then. I'm sick of looking at it."

After finishing their coffees, they got dressed and headed outside.

Lora's heart pounded so loudly she feared Randy would hear it. She also worried about the sound of the buzzing tipping him off, and she spoke quickly as they walked, hoping to distract him.

"You know, after we fix it, we ought to sand and stain it, or even paint it. I saw a real pretty teal birdhouse once, and I'm sure the birds don't care what color it is. If we hang it up in view of the windows, we can watch them coming and going in the morning. Wouldn't that be nice? We could get them a feeder. Oh, and a bird bath! I love watching them take a bath."

They'd made it to the birdhouse. Randy unceremoniously leaned down and picked it up.

"Damn, this thing's heavy," he muttered.

"Randy," Lora said, hit by a sudden wave of dread. It wasn't too late to stop him.

As if on cue, a single bee flew out of the round opening.

"Shit!" Randy threw the box to the ground.

The weakened wood exploded on impact, revealing the writhing hive inside. It was massive, taking up the entire contents of the birdhouse. A swarm, thick and black as smoke unfurled from the broken box and engulfed the couple angrily. Lora screamed. Randy bellowed as he fell to the ground, yelling her name and commanding her to help him. Stingers perforated Lora's body, a thousand needle pricks. She flailed her arms, but her efforts did nothing against the cloud of bees.

Lora's tongue began to swell in her mouth. It was getting harder to breathe. She'd been blinded, her eyelids too swollen to open, and her thoughts grew hazy. She collapsed beside her husband. Her first bee sting. In her last living moments, Lora realized that she was allergic, too.

***

When her eyes opened to soft white light, Lora felt a surge of relief. Someone must have called an ambulance just in time, and she'd been rushed to a hospital.

A sound crept into her consciousness. A deep, muffled humming, like a motor purring underwater. It sounded familiar, but she couldn't remember how. As she awoke, she became aware of her body, and realized she was on her side, curled into the fetal position. Disoriented, she looked down and was surprised to find herself totally nude. There were no tubes running into or out of her, no beeping machines, nothing to indicate that this was a hospital. It was more of a tiny, featureless cell.

The shape of the room was oddly geometric, with lots of sharp corners and edges. The white walls looked cushioned, and when Lora pressed her palm into one it left an oily imprint of her hand. Wax. She looked around. There were no doors. She was encased in the strange wax cell.

Lora felt the first twinge of panic. Growing frantic, she ran her hands around the interior of the room, searching for any means of escape, and gasped when her hands sank into one of the walls easily. When she brought her fingers to her face for inspection they were coated in thick, greasy wax. With newfound hope she noticed that this wall had a gentle glow compared to the others, hinting at light on the other side. This was the way out.

She knelt before the glowing surface and dug with both hands. As she pulled handful after handful of wax from the wall, the humming outside grew louder and deeper until the waves of it rattled her bones. Less muffled now, it sounded like a roaring engine. She knew that whatever was on the other side of the wall was powerful and large. When her hands broke through the last thin membrane she was hit with the full volume of the noise, and then she remembered. She knew that sound well.

Bees.

Lora crawled out of the cell, coating her face and body in sticky wax as she went. The buzzing engulfed her, and as her body stumbled onto the ground below, she sensed enthusiastic response in the makers of the noise. The sound rose and fell as it swirled around her.

Her limbs too shaky to stand, she remained on her knees. Wax coated her face, preventing her from seeing or speaking. She tried wiping it away, but her hands were also coated, rendering her efforts futile.

Suddenly, she felt the touch of countless thin appendages running over every curve of her body. Some were hard and bony, and scraped purposefully across her skin, removing wax in sheets. Others felt meaty and sticky, licking away residue. Still others were feather soft as they ran up and down her body in an exploratory, curious fashion.

They cleaned her face last, and when she finally opened her eyes, she screamed.

The creatures that surrounded her were neither human nor insect, but a hybrid of sorts. A sea of bulbous compound eyes regarded her with alien intelligence. The build of their bodies was distinctly masculine, with broad shoulders and wide chests that tapered into compact waistlines. They towered over Lora, standing at least seven feet tall atop rigid segmented legs that glinted in the light. Their chests were coated in fine yellow hairs, but their stomachs were bare, revealing six plates of dark exoskeleton that slid across one another like finely tuned muscles. Each creature had four arms ending in hooked claws, many of which still had traces of wax sticking to them from cleaning Lora's body. A set of glassy wings protruded from behind them, which they used in conversation. One would buzz his wings briefly, and another nearby would buzz in response. In addition, a pair of feathery antennae extended from each head, twitching in a silent communique. They were all talking about her.

Lora's eyes fell to a stinger. Until this moment they had been concealed. At rest, the bottom portion of the hybrids' bodies jutted out behind them, a huge mass of black and yellow muscle. But one of the creatures had folded his lower body forward to protrude from between his legs in an obviously lewd gesture. The stinger extended from the end, a thick, phallic, permanently erect appendage. He bobbed his stinger up and down at Lora, his buzz rising and falling with the movement of his cock. A fat drop of amber sap hung from its tip.

Her eyes widened. She knew she should be terrified, but excitement surged through her veins like an electric current. The swarm stared at her hungrily. They wanted her, and they wanted her to know it. One of them unrolled a long, black tongue from his mouth and ran it up her cheek. The swarm buzzed, excited. A fog of animal lust was palpable in the air.

She took in their surroundings. They were in a beehive, with walls of interlocking hexagonal cells that stretched as high as she could see. All were empty, waiting. The hive was ready for the next brood. Lora knew that male bees who mated were called drones and decided that's what these creatures were.

A drone put two claws beneath each of her arms and pulled her into a standing position. She clutched onto him, still wobbling, and dug her fingers into the hair on his chest. He smelled like pollen, like sunshine. He wrapped his arms around Lora and squeezed her against his chest in a tight hug. Then they were in flight, her feet dangling freely. The sound of his beating wings purred against her body, and Lora felt plates of exoskeleton sliding against her skin as he maneuvered through the air. He was strong, carrying her with ease. She felt safe in his arms.

They didn't travel far before landing in front of a large rectangular block. Made of the same white wax as her cell, it rose from the ground and reached to just below waist level of the drones. It looked like an altar. The swarm crowded around, and Lora understood.

Her temples pulsed with adrenaline. A gang bang. She had never had one before, but it was one of her deepest fantasies. To be lavished with the desire of so many men would be a dream come true. But there were so many of them, and they were so much bigger and stronger than she. Did she dare?

The altar came to her shoulders. She tried hoisting herself up, but after a few seconds of clumsy struggling, a drone lifted her by the ass until she could scramble atop the ivory surface. He let his hand slide over Lora's body as he pulled it away, and she shuddered. For all their strength, their touches had been so gentle.

The packed wax felt cool against her hot skin, and she lay on her back to savor it. The swarm circled the altar, looking down at her. One of them leaned forward and ran his feathery antennae down her body. Their feelers were silky soft, and her skin goose bumped with pleasure in response. The others followed suit, caressing her in the same way. She shivered with delight as the swarm lightly tickled her entire body. Soon enough a few began to focus on the triangle of her pubic area, and the light flicking of her labia and clitoral hood made Lora squirm. Others tickled her hardening nipples, making her breath quicken. Lora felt her pussy moisten and spread her legs, inviting them to explore deeper.

"More," she sighed. "I want more."

On her command, a tongue slid up the crease of her thigh, and she gasped in surprise. Again, the others followed, licking her together. Tongues slid back and forth across her nipples and teased around her dripping pussy. One found Lora's mouth and she kissed it back, her eyes closed. A number of tongues licked up and down either side of her twat, a cruel torment. After a few painful seconds of teasing, a tongue centered over her clit, moving in steady circles.

"Yes," she sighed.

A second tongue entered her forcefully. She writhed and moaned, the long tongue filling her completely, the sensation of its movements inside her driving her crazy.

"Please, please fuck me," she said.

She watched a drone at her feet fold his stinger forward and press it into the mound of her cunt. With his cock wedged between her fleshy lips, he buzzed.

The resulting vibration was so strong, so total that she screamed in surprise and her legs bucked violently. In one smooth motion, he slipped inside of her soaking pussy and she shrieked as if she were being butchered. His cock stretched her to full capacity. It hurt in the best way, and she began to work herself up and down the length of it with her teeth bared.

It was then that they swarmed her, their buzzing feverish. The drones took turns pumping into every hole, every crevice of her body. Her mouth stretched wide and dripped with thick drool as a succession of cocks used it hungrily. They fought over her pussy, pushing one another aside and pumping greedily until another demanded his turn. Others used her clenched fists, her feet, and straddled her tits, squeezing them around their girth. Many of them merely beat themselves off with four hooked hands, watching the spectacle.

Lora had never felt so worshipped. The overstimulation sent rocking waves of pleasure through her, and they crashed more and more frequently in the rising storm of her pussy. Her body quaked as she edged toward climax, her clit buzzing, until at long last it erupted out of her in a geyser of ecstasy, and she screamed.

As she came the first spurt hit her mouth, hot and heavy. The load was so sticky that for a moment her lips were glued shut. Lora forced her tongue between her lips to taste it. Honey.

She felt another cum inside of her from behind, filling her with hot sap. The rest of the swarm came in unison, jerking themselves onto every inch of her skin. Streams of honey jetted across her until they melded together in a single sticky coating. Lora sucked it from her fingers. She looked like a trophy, golden and shiny from head to toe. She felt like one, too.

Four drones lifted her gingerly from the altar and stood her back on the ground. Ahead, she saw a crew put the finishing touches on a grand wax chair. A throne, she realized. She had performed well. She had been accepted.

She took her seat and regarded the hive with pride. *A queen,* she thought. *Royalty.* A smile curved on her mouth, her giddiness straining against the cooling honey on her face. She could get used to this.

A lurch in her gut made her bend forward. Her insides gurgled. She looked down, and her eyes widened.

Her belly was swelling, inflating like a balloon. She pressed her hands against the growing mound of her stomach, applying futile pressure. Another painful lurch, an angry groan from her guts. A gurgling mass expanded inside of her, growing heavier as it forced her skin to stretch. Lora recognized the taut, distended shape of her belly as a late-term pregnancy. From within, something moved. A whine escaped her mouth.

"No, no, no."

It kept growing. As the delicate flesh of her belly was stretched paper thin, she made out a quivering beneath the surface, as if something was straining toward the light of the hive.

She screamed as a ribbon of red popped into view. Her skin had split down the curve of her belly. As the first gash widened, a smaller one appeared on her side. It was going to burst through her gut like an alien, she realized. Lora knew nothing of childbirth, but a primal lobe of her brain screamed an internal command: *PUSH*.

Gritting her teeth, she obeyed. The thing inside of her contorted in response, elongated. It brought mild relief, and she did it again. It pressed against her pelvis, meeting resistance. She held the pressure, willing the parasite away from her stomach.

"Get out of me!" she spat and gave a final desperate push.

A geyser of larvae exploded out of her like a popped pimple, the force of it blowing through her, splitting her from hole to hole. She shrieked as it spattered the wax with maggots and slime, filling her ears with the sound of heavy rain. Her stomach deflated as the last of them made an exodus out of her ruined cunt. Her children writhed all around her, white and segmented. She moaned.

Still sitting in the throne, Lora looked down at herself. The honey had held her together. Her wounds tingled with a familiar sensation, like a limb that was coming back to life after falling asleep. They were healing quickly. Soon she would be good as new.

In a daze, she looked around. The drones worked, picking up the larvae and depositing them into cells. Once a baby was nestled in place, the drone would heave up a blob of soft, greasy wax to cap them inside. One-by-one the cells were filled from the ground up. As far as Lora could tell, they never ended. They towered above her forever, growing up into eternity.

The drones had made quick work of the first batch, and the hive floor was almost free from larvae. A congregation began to form at the altar again, each drone taking a place there as he finished his share of the work. From their body language and the lazy movements of their antennae they seemed to be engaging in the sort of mindless chit-chat one does while in wait. They paid her no mind now; she had served her purpose and was of no use to them until she returned to the altar. She felt the sting of rejection and sneered. Lora had suffered many cruelties in her time but being ignored was a first.

A throne, an altar, and a tower of cells were the only contents of the hive. There was nowhere else to go. She could enjoy the throne for a while, sure. But sooner or later she'd need them again, and they knew it. They would wait her out. They would make her choose.

Perhaps all of this was temporary, she reasoned. If she fulfilled her duties and replenished the hive, then they'd worry less about making babies and more about her. The cells had to end eventually; they couldn't *really* go on forever.

Let's get this over with.

Lora rose on unsteady limbs and took a shaky step toward the altar. They turned to face her, and her spirits soared.

FIVE NIGHTS WITH TEDDY

THURSTON HOWL

—THE FIRST NIGHT—

I'D HEARD WHISPERS of the place for months, a guy who could really turn you into your fursona. I wasn't what's called a therian. I didn't believe I was a cow or a pig or anything like that. But . . . I still wanted to *be* my fursona. I hated the way I looked. Too big. Too hairy. My eyes crossed, and my dick was a meager four inches. My fursona on the other hand—or paw—was Adonis. You know, if Adonis was an anthropomorphic wolf.

I looked down at the map on my phone to make sure this was the right place. Yeah . . . it was. This decrepit warehouse was it. Might have been part of a factory at one point, but now all the windows were boarded, with yellow caution tape around the doors. Even the parking lot was mostly a pile of rubble; the streetlights once pooling amber light over it, but now those too were dim. But there, in a far corner of the building, there was a light on. I *was* expected.

I swallowed nervously before turning off the car and getting out. I left my phone there but brought my keys and wallet with me. The only other thing I had with me was the picture of my fursona. It was a muscly gray wolf with stark white eyes. No irises or pupils. It was a nude reference sheet, so the character's knotted cock hung a good ten inches. I had sent the mysterious Teddy a couple of images already, but he had asked I bring the printed sheet too. Something he could put up as a reference while he worked on me. Five nights with him, and my dreams could come true. Five nights with him, and I could *be* Dante.

By the time I made it over the piles of rubble to the entrance nearest the light, I was exhausted. I knocked twice on the door and waited. Rather than Teddy coming to the door, the door just . . . opened. I heard a voice from behind the boarded entrance: "You can duck under the boards. Come on in, Dante."

My heart leaped at the use of my furry name. I gathered my wits and crouched as low as I could, barely squeezing under the boards and making it out the other side. The room was small. Loose fur covered the floor. The walls were yellow with large holes here and there, leading to other darkened rooms. The place smelled . . . oddly sterile. In the back was a hospital bed, and sitting beside that was a bear. I'm not talking about a guy with a comical bear fursuit. I mean, it looked like an actual bear. I jumped back, and the bear opened its mouth.

"Surprised?" it said. "I'm Teddy."

My jaw hung for a moment before I stepped forward, pointing a finger at him. "You're . . . I'll look that realistic?"

The bear grunted.

"Wow," I said. While I liked many of the toonier fursuits, what attracted me most were the realistic ones, those that looked like what anthropomorphic animals would be if they were real.

"You bring the ref sheet?" he asked, pointing to a corkboard beside the bed. The board was empty except for a few colorful tacks pressed into it.

"Uh, yeah." I came closer and offered the bear the sheet of paper.

He looked it over for a few seconds before standing on his hind paws and pinning the sheet to the board. I admired my lupine body on the sheet. It had both my anthro form and my feral form. The former was sexy; the latter majestic, as any good wolf should be. "Great, now, first, you have the money, yeah?"

My heart froze. Had I forgotten it? I pressed a hand against my back pocket and found my wallet. "Oh, yeah, here." I handed him the hundred-dollar bills. I felt a lump in my throat at giving him so much money. Way more than the cost of a fursuit. But, if I looked as good as he did, boy would this be worth it.

"Next," his growling voice said, "I need you to sign some paperwork." He handed me a small sheaf of papers, about ten pages. It was a contract. Most of it was disclaimers and liability clauses. Basically, if I wasn't happy with how I turned out, I couldn't ask for

a refund or something like that. At least, that's what the first couple of pages looked like. Seemed like basic stuff for something like this. I knew what I was getting into, and I couldn't hold him responsible for any accidents. I skipped through a few pages and signed the final page with the pen he offered, then handed it back to him.

Teddy seemed like the kind of person I couldn't trust that much, granted. After all, how many anthro bears do most people know? But then again, I didn't trust most people. I had seen a couple of pictures of Teddy's "patients" though. I knew he could do it. I had spoken with old friends of his back before his transformation, and they attested to his good nature. I believed them.

"Great. Lie on the bed." His voice was gruff, low and menacing.

I did as he said. It was a firm mattress, far from comfortable, and I folded my hands over my stomach. "Now what?"

He pulled a gas mask out from behind the head of the bed and pulled it over my face. "Now, I need you to just breathe. Can you do that, Dante?"

I smiled up at him and breathed. I felt the gas in my lungs instantly. This was much more potent than the stuff you get at the dentist. But as my vision began to fade, I caught a detail I hadn't noticed before. The bear's face leaned closer, and I saw the stitches near his eye sockets, where the skin of a real bear had been sewn onto his human skin. But it was too late for my body to resist anymore, and my mind went screaming into the depths of darkness. I was only vaguely aware of my clothing being cut off my body.

—THE SECOND NIGHT—

I woke up with my entire body itching. Imagine a swarm of mosquitos crawling all over you, and then biting you at once. Then imagine the bites swelling against each other. Or better yet, a few hundred fuzzy spiders crawling sluggishly across your body. It felt like that. And it really was everywhere: between my toes, over my ears, under my balls, between my ass cheeks. Everywhere.

I lifted a hand to scratch, but my hand only rose an inch. I turned my head and opened my eyes. There was a wolf's arm beside me, manacled to the bed. As I tried to pull away from it, my wrist strained against the manacles—it was *my* arm. I looked down. There was silver and black fur all the way down my body. My penis, thankfully, looked fine, and—I was naked. I desperately wished to cover myself up from the bear looming over the edge of the bed, but both my wrists and ankles were strapped to the bed, a manacle at each corner.

"What is it, Dante?" the growl asked. "You look concerned, or stressed, at least." The bear stood upright, paws holding the metal edge of the bed. The bed was so low to the ground, he looked much taller than he actually was. "What's the matter?" he repeated, almost leaning over the bed now. The room smelled worse than it had yesterday. Like blood . . . and burning flesh. What had happened in just a day? "Dante?"

My eyes were wide with fright as I swallowed, feeling my Adam's apple bob against a manacle at my throat. "I-I'm scared. What happened? M-My whole body feels like it's being covered with ants. It hurts." I couldn't help myself. I started shaking. My eyes kept darting across the room but only found shadows and a singular lamp, its warm light catching in the bear's cold eyes. "P-Please stop. Let me out. It hurts."

He smirked and then walked over to the corkboard. With a paw, he gestured to my ref sheet. "Look at that wolf. He's so sexy. He's happy, too. Do you want to quit already? You've just started. All I've done is given you some fur. Look."

I looked back at my fur. It was indeed the exact same color as Dante's. It hit me how he gave me the fur though. He sewed it on me. He used fur and a needle and gave it to me like it was a full-body tattoo. My whole body looked like this now.

"See how beautiful you are? Do you really want me to take the time to undo all my hard work already?"

I shook my head slowly. While he was talking, I didn't think so much about the itching. Don't get me wrong. It was there. But I could distance myself a bit. Just a bit. "H-How much more of this? I-I'm not sure how much I can take. But . . . I want to keep going. I don't want you to stop." I clenched my fists. "Don't stop."

He laughed then. "Good boy." He ruffled my head fur—*I have head fur!*—and smiled. "Alright, then. But are you sure? This is your last chance. After the second night, I don't let my patients leave till I'm completely finished. Understand?"

"Yes . . . " I started. "I'm sure." I was far from it. But I wanted this. I *needed* this. I couldn't stop now. I wouldn't. "Just . . . if you can make it less painful . . . please do."

He walked back to the end of the bed and leaned forward, his large head inches over my exposed cock. His claws raked carefully through the fur on my thighs. Despite myself, my cock twitched. It started getting hard, and I blushed beneath the mask of fur sewn onto my face. "So . . . out of curiosity . . . what's Dante into?" Despite the realism of the bear's face and snout, he seemed to emote a wicked smirk.

"W-What do you mean?" I didn't remember this being in the contract at all.

"I mean, you must have lots of art made of Dante, right? Surely, you've had NSFW art made. What all is Dante into?" Teddy kept stroking the insides of my thighs, never touching my cock or balls but always getting dangerously close.

I nod. "Yeah, I've had s-some art commissioned. He's a subby, kinky wolf. Thought it would be f-fun to have a sub wolf as opposed to the u-usual dom wolf. B-b-but I'm not like that at all. I'm just a top . . . and pretty vanilla in real life. You know?" I could feel my heart racing in my chest. I wasn't used to even talking about stuff like this, but Teddy didn't seem to be the kind of bear you said no to.

"No worries. Get comfortable, pup. Let's get you back under so you don't have to put up with the itching as much."

Thank god, I thought.

"Have a good sleep, Dante."

As he leaned over me to grab the gas mask to place back over my face, I felt his cock brush against mine, and I almost yelped. But the sweet smell of the gas was just . . . intoxicating. I felt him grab the fur between my ears as he continued grinding against me, and my flesh there exploded with searing pain. I heard him say, "Let's see how strong this fur is . . . " But I was already fading.

—THE THIRD NIGHT—

While the itchiness throughout my skin had abated, my entire head felt like it was on fire. It wasn't an itching pain, just a sharp one, like knives digging into my cheekbones and lower jaw. My ears felt both numb and on fire, and the pain worked its way across my eyes and up my skull. I tried to raise a hand to touch my face, but the manacle around my wrist was an acute reminder of where I was. *What had happened this time?* I thought. *How am I different now? Is it done? Am I Dante? Is he going to stop the pain now?*

My eyelids flickered open, but everything was still dark. Maybe Teddy was out of the room and had left the lights off? Then, I heard movement. The clattering of metal tools. The shuffling of heavy, furred paws. The creaking of floorboards beneath a bear's weight. I tapped my paw against the side of the bed, desperate to get his attention, my head swimming with both pain and confusion. *Why can't I see? Is it really pitch black in here?*

"Oh Dante, are you awake?" The voice was a low growl, but it seemed pleased, as if the operation had gone as planned. "I figured you'd wake up at some point before I get started on the next phase. About time, wolf. How are you feeling?"

I whined loud and tried to form words, but nothing came. My throat roared with pain, but the only sound that escaped my mouth was that high whine. I tried harder, trying to form the word, "*help,*" but the whine just grew louder. My mouth felt . . . different. Cumbersome, thick, sluggish. I forced sound out more, desperate to make at least one coherent word. The sound rose in my chest and escaped my maw:

A howl. I couldn't speak, but I could howl. This wasn't some weak imitation. It sounded like a real wolf howl. It *felt* like a real wolf howl.

Teddy laughed. I could imagine his fur rippling with each full-bodied chuckle. I heard his footsteps approach the side of the bed. "Good boy! How did your first howl feel?" I was dumbfounded. What had he done to me? As if in answer to my question, he said, "Real wolves can't talk, Dante. You know that. I had to cut out your vocal cords. Implant those that are more similar to a wolf's. And, of course, get you a full snout."

I struggled.

"And, I was looking closer at your image of Dante. He didn't have any pupils. So neither do you now!" He ruffled my head fur, and the sheer pain almost sent me back into the darkness. "And removing those old human ears and replacing them with a wolf's. We're over halfway done, Dante!"

I kept struggling against the bonds. I wanted out. This had gone too far. Yes, I wanted to look like my fursona, to *become* my fursona, but I had still wanted to be able to talk, for God's sake. I still wanted to *see*. He had to fix it. He had to give me my sight and speech back. This wasn't what I had agreed to. I let out another howl.

I felt a claw trace its way up my navel, parting my fur as it went. I shivered and tried to arch my body away from the touch, but I could only move so much, and the claw continued its upward trajectory. "Oh, stop worrying so much. The pain won't last forever. I promise. And by then, you really will be Dante. Your true wolf self. You're getting so close. Besides . . . it's too late to turn back now."

I felt a hand clamp down around my mouth—my *snout*. My first thought was that he was going to choke me. It felt so odd, having bones that extended so far past my face, and my nose was at the tip of that structure. Even with my mouth held shut, I could breathe fine. "Such a lovely snout," Teddy whispered. "Now, let's see how submissive my new wolf is."

The bed creaked. I could feel it creaking. He was stepping onto the bed. The weight was placed on either side of my head. Was he standing over me? A few seconds passed.

What felt like a bucket of cold slime poured over my muzzle. The smell was chemical and faintly sweet. I coughed as the sticky goo pooled into my nostrils. It lathered my face, sticking my fur in clumps and eventually trailing its way down into my eyes. Then, something warm, wet, and fleshy pressed against my nose. It didn't have much structure, but smoother, fatty flesh also pressed around my snout.

"So," he said above me, "let's see if you lick tail like other dogs."

I kept my mouth closed. That was his . . . *tailhole*? No, I refused.

"Aw, c'mon, Dante. You resist, and I'll just make you do it."

Even as I tried to open my mouth to protest, the bear lowered himself over me, his tailhole stretching slowly over my snout, the lube on my snout easing his descent. My flesh erupted with itching sensations, and my skull felt like it was being hammered into, the bone structure still fresh. His hole kept stretching, until my snout was a good three inches inside him. The musk was tolerable, but I couldn't breathe at all. Knowing that either his balls or his tail were hanging over my blank eyes just made me squirm harder, much to his pleasure.

"Aw, looks like the wolfie is enjoying this," he said with an audible smirk. My cock indeed felt hard, but I didn't care about shame right now. I wanted him to get off. It hurt more than it humiliated. At this point, I would do anything to stop the pain, even if my cock was into this.

I whined into him, and my chest started heaving. My lungs tightened, and my heartbeat pounded in my ears. I struggled harder, desperate to breathe in air. But he just kept lowering his weight onto me, my snout now pushing six or seven inches into him. Then, I felt his rough, leathery paw squeeze around my cock. I made a muffled yelp in his hole, but my vision started getting fuzzy. My head was killing me.

"Just a little longer . . . " he moaned.

The darkness started to pixelate. I felt warm, thick liquid splatter against my stomach. I felt it pool in my belly button. It was not my cum. It was his.

"Ffffuck," I heard him whisper, and he leaned back on top of my snout. The pain that movement sent through my head made the darkness turn red and then white.

—THE FOURTH NIGHT—

I was never the kind of person who was squeamish when it came to body modification. Before I had even heard of Teddy, I had gotten a couple of tattoos, a wolf on my back and a Celtic symbol on my forearm. I had both my ears pierced, and I wasn't even afraid of needles. While other people my age would make fun of older generation celebrities who had plastic surgery to preserve their youth, I saw them as paragons of beauty. I had been raised to believe my body was a temple, but, over the years, I came to see it more as a superchurch, ever in need of upgrades. And Dante—he was the ultimate purchase. He was a pinnacle that most plastic surgeons had shaken their heads at me for, denying me the chance to have such an operation. They had said they couldn't or wouldn't do it. Many warned that, not only would it be hard to integrate into society, but the daily pain of things as mundane as walking would make life unbearable.

So, when I came to on the fourth night, I was mentally able to know the pain I was feeling meant some new physical modification—the more I hurt, the better I must look. The monstrous Teddy had altered my skin to be fur, my mouth to be a snout, my eyes to be blank, and my ears to be lupine. Yet for all I hurt and suffered these feelings of helpless at my inability to see or speak, I was curious. What was different? How was I improved tonight?

What hurt this time though wasn't my skin or my bones or my eyes or my jaw: it was my dick. I could feel it against my stomach, at least twice its usual length now and with a knot, too. My balls felt larger between my legs, and, further down than that, I had a tail. I could *feel* it, not just against my legs, no; the tail itself had nerves. I could move it around. But all of these modifications hurt like hell. They itched and burned, and I wished Teddy could just saw them off. The skin under my fur blushed at the mental image I had of what my cock must look like, if it really indeed looked like Dante's. It was one of the few characteristics that was the same on both the anthropomorphic and feral versions of the wolf on the ref sheet. Dante was hung . . . *I* was hung.

Aside from all the pain though, it felt *swollen*. It felt like the worst case of blue balls I'd ever had. I wanted to jack—paw—off *now*. My wrists pulled on the manacles, hoping they were magically gone now and I could stroke myself to completion, but, no, I was still bound. God, my cock and balls itched so much yet felt so much need to be caressed, I wish I could have masturbated with a sheet of sandpaper. Surely that could have alleviated the insufferable combination of itch and need. I tried to move my thighs around my erection, hoping maybe I could trap my erection between my legs and stroke it that way, but my legs too were restrained too tightly.

The bear snickered in the darkness . "Having fun, pup?"

I whined and then barked, my body struggling against the chains and my hips bucking forward. I was angry. I was needy. I was in pain. I tried to communicate somehow that I wanted him to let me go, right then and there. I gestured to the manacles with my nose. I clanked and pulled on the chains. I put all my energy into rocking the bed. Everything to relay that I wanted out.

His paw on my cock was what calmed me. It felt like a cool beverage on a warm summer's day. He started pumping his closed fist up and down my enormous length. "You like that, Dante? You've got a whole twelve inches on you now . . . plus a knot . . . bigger balls . . . and a nice, fluffy tail. You're becoming quite the handsome wolf."

My tongue splayed out of my mouth as I panted. I couldn't help it. It felt so good, and he just kept pumping for a solid ten minutes. I felt *so* close, and yet I wasn't cumming. I whined, and my ears naturally flattened. I wanted to cum so badly. My body temperature felt higher than I had ever felt it, like I was getting high as balls from my own endorphins. But nothing was happening.

"That's right, pup," the bear growled. His tongue flicked across my sensitive and tapered tip, teasing me. "Subby pups like you don't get to cum." He sucked on my first couple of inches and then pulled back. "Or orgasm." He pushed his head down half my length before coming up again. "You're my bottom bitch now, Dante. You can piss just fine with this. But actually cumming? Not gonna happen. Felt no need to reattach that tube with the surgery." He laughed. It was a deep, throaty laugh. Malicious. Sinister. Then, I heard him lick his lips.

I whimpered as loudly as I was able without forcing my throat. I tried thrusting up again toward his face. He had to be lying. He couldn't do that to me. That had to be a breach of our contract or something. Or maybe . . . maybe I needed to just obey. If I did whatever he said, maybe he'd let me go. That was it. That *had* to be it. I just had to quit resisting so much. I lay flat against the bed and fought the urge to buck. Little shivers of desperation crept along my spine, but I stayed still.

He squeezed my knot hard and *tsk*ed. "That's a good boy. You know fighting me won't do you much good. Now, let's give you a little reward. Something before I put you back under."

I heard him move and fumble with something metallic on his person. Next thing I knew, he was unlocking the manacles. I felt the heavy circles of metal fall away from my ankles, then my wrists. But, as he started to remove the restraints, he turned my body so I was on my stomach. He was *positioning* me. I was standing on my hands and knees on the bed. Then, I felt the manacles clamp back over each limb. I was tempted to resist when it came to my last ankle, but I remembered what he said. He's rewarding me.

Still, I was confused: if he wasn't setting me free, what was he doing? Was he just wanting to check me out to make sure I looked good from behind too? Maybe under surgery, he hadn't been able to really turn me over well, so he didn't know what I looked like from all angles yet? I felt him grab my tail roughly and lift it. My tailhole puckered instantly, and I blushed. Was he . . . examining my tail? Then, a fleshy tip touched my tailhole, and I almost jumped. There was silence for a few seconds. I started counting . . . *One . . . two . . . three . . . four . . . five . . . six . . .*

He rammed his dry cock deep in me, one single thrust, and I howled, my throat cracking instantly. He leaned over me so his gut lay across my back, and his balls slapped against mine with his deep thrust. Before I could recover from the sudden shock of having my anal virginity so painfully ravaged, he pulled out and thrust again. Like my itching/needing cock, this feeling was an uncomfortable mixture of pain and pleasure. I wanted him to *Stop! For the love of God!* and I wanted him to *Fuck me harder! Please, I feel so close!*

Before I could howl again, he wrapped a heavy, sweat-slick paw over my snout, a furry muzzle. He was strong. He clamped my mouth shut easily, and his claws invaded my nostrils. I couldn't breathe, but he kept thrusting. My tailhole felt raw and sore, but my cock throbbed every time the bear hilted himself inside me. My consciousness once again started slipping.

"That's my good bitch," I heard him say through the fog. Before I faded, I felt his cock spurt his warm, wet spunk inside me, and my hole clenched around him. He stayed inside for a few seconds, and then emptied his bladder into my rectum. He groaned and said, "One more night, pup." I retched into his paw and passed out.

—THE FIFTH NIGHT—

Pain wasn't what woke me on the fifth night; it was revulsion. My new, sharper nose picked up too many scents at once: piss, shit, semen, and lots of wet dog. I was lying on cold linoleum, and the walls reverberated with sound: barks, growls, and the obnoxiously loud dripping of water. But there was one familiar scent before me, a few feet away: Teddy.

"Hey, Dante, how you feeling?" the bear said, his voice laced with what seemed genuine concern. "Believe it or not, the operation's complete . . . You're officially Dante. However, there are a uh . . . couple of things we should probably talk about." The voice was devoid of his usual smirk. It was far from submissive or ashamed. But it was still cautious. "You're a bit more doped up than usual for this. Pups in the past have uh . . . hurt themselves after hearing."

I felt others around me. They were furry. Their bodies occasionally brushed past me. Some smaller than me, some bigger. Occasionally, a wet nose would press against my face, belly, or tail and sniff. I didn't move. Had Teddy brought other canines to me? Was this some kind of test? A test for me? What did he expect of me?

"It's uh . . . about that contract you signed. There are a couple of things. First, uh . . . the contract states the ref sheet you brought as the main document for surgery. Which means . . . I had the ultimate say over which form you kept as your transformed state. And I uh . . . well . . . "

My mind felt foggy. Slow. But even then, I tried to feel along my body for what was different. It didn't take long. My limbs. They were all bent at weird angles. They hurt like hell. But it was a muted hell. My limbs had all turned digitigrade.

"I went with your feral form." He giggled to himself. "I can't very well have an anthro pup, you know?"

I didn't know. I didn't understand what was happening. I had survived all five nights, right? I was free to go, right?

As if sensing my confusion, he continued, "And uh . . . the other thing. One of the last pages of the contract . . . it basically means I'm now your uh . . . legal guardian. Or well . . . was . . . While you've been out, I've been taking care of other paperwork. As far as the state is concerned, you're effectively dead."

I heard the sound of nails being hammered into my coffin in my head. I whined and yelped as I struggled to stand on my new limbs. I had to get away. I had to escape. No, this had to be some dream, some twisted, drug-induced nightmare. I had to wake up. I had to get back home. I wobbled on my legs and stumbled forward a few steps on all fours, my legs crossing at one point.

"Hey, pup, I wouldn't try moving so fast if I were you. They can smell your—" My ears pricked as I felt the surrounding forms press closer. Some nipped at my heels; some at my neck. I ended up toppling over one of them and landing on top. "—submission."

The animal I landed on wrapped its large paws around me. My chest pressed against its, and my groin against its tummy . . . Then I felt his dick pressing against my tailhole. I didn't have the energy to yelp again, though my heart was hammering in my head. Everything still felt slow. The canid's cock pressed into me roughly, and I felt the soreness from when Teddy had fucked me the night before, but the cock pressed in nevertheless.

"The less you resist the easier it'll be for you. I promise." The bear's words were far from reassuring. Yet, even now, my cock was hard and throbbing against the lower canine's stomach. "You'll get used to it. You don't have to worry about family shit, work, school, none of that. You're free down here."

Another of the animals mounted me from behind, and my eyes, though blank, went wide with fear. Despite the wag of my hips in trying to escape, this canine too pushed his cock in above the other's, and both cocks thrust at different speeds into me. I could feel my hole bleeding around them, and tears filled my eyes. But my cock kept grinding against the lower canine's stomach, desperate for an impossible release. I had no way of knowing if these canines were real animals or the Frankenstein animals Teddy had created. If I could see them, would they all have human eyes looking back at me through fur sewn into their skin? Would I see human limbs broken and reworked into digitigrade segments? What humanity was left? What humanity was left in me?

"Life as Teddy's pup isn't so bad though. Some of the guys here have lived with me for six or seven years already. I'll be down to feed you daily and get you water and all kinds of stuff. You'll see. You'll learn to love it." I heard Teddy start to move. I heard him jangle some keys. He was leaving. But I couldn't move. I was trapped.

A third canid stood before me and then placed his paws over my head toward the back of my shoulder blades, and his cock pressed against my lips. In trying to yelp in resistance, the canid thrust forward, his cock filling my snout till the knot bumped my nose.

"But if there's one thing you should remember . . . " the bear started. I heard a metal gate closing near him, and his voice became more distant. I was so lost in the heat of this furred orgy, I almost didn't hear his final words: " . . . you'll always be my little Dante."

Over time, the pain would fade. The wounds would heal. The memories of what I was before Dante too would fall into darkness. And he was right. At the end of the day, I would always be Dante. His Dante. And every night I spent beneath Teddy's factory reminded me how lucky a wolf I really was.

And five nights would blur into five weeks . . . and five months . . . and five years . . .

Oh Piggy, My Piggy

MATT SCOTT

I **FOUND TWO THINGS** disturbingly disconcerting about hearing my name called from beside me as I slept. I don't know how I really knew this at the time; I was in bed, on my back, eyes closed (of course), and was somewhere in between restlessness and REM sleep, but I knew Potter was calling my name as if to rouse me from my slumber. The first thing that bothered me about that was that Potter was not allowed in our room after bedtime. We kept the door shut for a reason. The second thing that was so perplexing about the gravel laden voice calling to me from out of the darkness, was that Potter is a pig.

I don't mean to say that Potter is sloppy or given to slovenly habits. Quite the contrary in fact. He is clean, well-groomed and pleasant smelling. I mean to say by calling him a pig, that he is, quite irrevocably, by nature and design, a swine. A potbellied if you like. To use a more apt colloquialism, Potter is our pet mini pig.

I was half asleep after all, and I suddenly realized that along with my name being spoken from out of the void, I also smelled smoke. This is what I believe truly motivated me to roll onto my side and face the edge of the bed and the strangeness that was beyond it. I blinked the sleep away as quickly as I could in a muddled rationalization that I had merely dreamt my name being said in a subconscious desire to wake and flee the inevitable inferno that was surely consuming the house.

However, instead of the orange glow snaking in from beneath the door from surreptitious flames licking the walls of the outer hallway, I was certainly more than surprised to see what had awoken me. It was no benevolent specter from the other side, warning me to grab what I could and save as many as I was able; nor was it a phantom advising me of visitors to come to show me the errors of my ways lest I be doomed to an eternity in the fiery pit. It is my contention that either of these two scenarios would have made more sense to me than what I laid there staring at in a somewhat incredulous fog.

"I'm hungry, John. You going to get up and make something or am I just going to start chewing on the mattress? Sticking my snout in the wet spot on Kelly's side" Potter motioned with his front hoof toward Kelly, my wife, who was fast asleep beside me in the bed, laying in the remnants of our love making hours earlier. Instead of changing the bedding, she had placed towels beneath her so as not be directly in the puddle we had made on the fitted sheet, too much effort after such a strenuous session. And besides, we weren't animals.

Staring dumfounded at Potter, I said, "What do you want me to fix?"

He took a drag from his cigarette, and I was amazed at the dexterity with which he manipulated his rather limited digits. For an ungulate, he seemed to be doing just fine.

"Pancakes?" He asked, sounding like a Jersey wise guy or an old-timesy villain from Atlantic City.

"What time is it?"

"Early, but I've been up a while. Got hungry." He blew a smoke ring that wafted toward my face and hovered in front of me.

"Ok," I said, and why not? You would think that I would have had more to say than that, more questions than a marathon of Jeopardy reruns, but I didn't. Not really. Not then. I got up, looking for my slippers beside the bed on the floor. Potter used his hind hoof and scooted them over to me. I slipped them on and led him out of the bedroom, down the hall, and into the kitchen where I flipped on the overhead light. He pulled a stool away from the center island and sat as I unhooked a skillet from the rack above and grabbed a large plastic mixing bowl from a cabinet beneath it.

"Cinnamon?" I asked as I reached for the spice rack above the stove.

"Yeah sure, put some of it in there," Potter replied and squashed out his cigarette on the side of his hoof. He crossed his two tiny forelimbs in front of him on the counter as if waiting for me to start asking questions. I was waiting too, though I was trying to word them properly. One never knows how situations like these will turn out.

I started with the most obvious. "So, how long have you been able to talk?" I poured the batter into the skillet. It slowly mixed with the olive oil that had been heating on the stove.

"Always could," he replied. "How long you been able to hear me?" He seemed agitated, and I could sense that maybe his feelings had been hurt by me not being able to understand him these past three years. "Never mind," he waved a hoof in the air as if brushing away the thought completely, "That's not why I woke you, though I am hungry. Worked up quite an appetite earlier."

"Yeah?"

"Yeah. It's what I wanted to talk to you about. Kelly would have too, but she wanted me to do it." He got up and went to the laptop. It was on the coffee table in the living room. A rectangular wooden piece of knotted walnut, sturdy and rustic. He sat down, flipped it open. "Here, this might help."

I turned the heat off on the stove and followed him out of the kitchen. The pancakes could wait. "Kelly knows about this? About you? I don't understand. What's this now?"

Kelly had gotten Potter as a rescue from a farm about five hours from our home. She had seen a post on Facebook about a litter of pot bellies an elderly couple had recently had on their small farm and they were unable to keep them. The couple seemed all too happy to rehome Potter when Kelly had inquired after him, and she drove up that weekend and brought him home the same night. He was no bigger than a kitten and looked as cute as a button. That was three years ago.

"Easy, big guy; deep breaths," he said, cueing a video to play on the laptop. "This is going to sting a bit."

The video file began to play. Kelly was sitting on the couch we now sat on, Potter and I. She was wearing the flowered print dress I bought her when we went to the little Bed and Breakfast in Rochester last year. Her legs crossed, her hands folded in her lap, she looked into the tiny camera on the top edge of the computer and started to speak.

"John, my love," she began, and I almost thought I saw her bottom lip quiver, just ever so slightly. Maybe? Maybe not. "First of all, honey, I want to say how much I love you. You are a great man, a good husband, and a dear friend."

Shit, this ain't good.

"I tell you these things so that you won't think this is your fault." I looked at the time stamp. Two hours ago. She made this tonight. We made love tonight. She got up after I went to sleep and came in here and recorded a goddamn dear john video after we had sex? What the fuck, man. I shifted in my seat and looked at Potter, who had paused the video sensing I needed a minute to process the information. Intuitive little guy. I'll give him that much.

He began to push play again on the mouse beside the laptop, but I stopped him.

"How? How do you know any of this?"

"Take a breath. There's more," is all he said, and clicked the tab on the mouse.

"Darling, when we met five years ago I was so taken with you. Your look, your touch, your zest for life, but after we married and moved out here, you became distant, moody, sullen. I know losing your job weighs heavily on you, it weighs on me too, but that's not it, is it?"

What the fuck was she saying? I do everything for that woman. I buy her candy and flowers, and dresses, and go to those stupid shops with her, and watch those stupid shows until I want to puke and punch her and them in the fucking face. What the holy fuck was she saying?

"It's the sex, John. You know it and I know it. You haven't gotten fully hard in a year and a half, and while we do other things that are fun—" she looked away from the camera as she said this, off screen, to her right, and blushed a little, the faintest of color flushing her cheeks, "—it just isn't enough. I need more. I need to be satisfied, John. I'm frustrated and tense all the time. I know this hurts, honey, but there is something you need to know."

I knew it. I fucking knew it.

Beside her in the video, on the floor next to the couch, was a bag, her overnight bag, the one she had taken with her to Rochester. I looked over to my left; it was still there. But she was in bed when

Potter came and got me. I'm sure of it. I went to get up, to go to her, to wake her and ask her what all this was about, but Potter stopped me.

"One more thing," he said, and let the video finish.

On the screen, another video popped up in the top right-hand corner, an overlay, picture in picture kind of thing. She continued talking as it played.

"Just so you know," she prefaced, "none of this was planned. It happened on its own and I want it to continue John. God, baby, I am so sorry. I love you. Goodbye." The little square in the top tight went full screen as she faded from view.

Kelly was naked, on her hands and knees, tits swinging back and forth, and Potter was pounding her from behind, huge corkscrew cock sliding in and out of her like a sick fun house gag. Except it was no gag. I could see the pleasure on her face as he bruised her ass with his body, his cock ramming home, touching parts of her I never knew she had. She was biting her bottom lip to keep from screaming, and when I thought she was going to, she flopped over to her back, spread her legs and waited with a glistening pussy as Potter unscrewed a jar of peanut butter and spread it over her vagina, her taint, her asshole. Then he buried his snout in there, working for his dinner. She let out a scream like I had never heard. Wait. Why didn't I hear it? Why didn't I know anything about it? Little bacon Bastard. Fuck him.

I was seeing red and sweating, my teeth clenched so tight I thought I was going to snap them off at the roots. Potter was up now, standing in front of me.

"There's more," he said.

Fuck more. I didn't want to see any more of this debaucherous shit. My wife, the pig fucker, fucking our now cognizant and quite verbose pig. Fuck this shit. But then, on the screen, Kelly began to scream louder, and not from pleasure. It sounded like pain. Like terror. Good. But I couldn't look away.

On the screen, Potter was biting her pussy, ripping it to shreds with his short tusks, nibbling her labia, tearing them from her body. Saliva gathered at the edges of his mouth as he went mad with hunger, rage, lust. Blood spurted from her mid-section as her intestines bubbled up to the surface of her abdomen, almost protruding, but not quite. Her legs kicked, then spasmed, her arms flailed then went slack. Blood ran from her mouth, dribbled down her chin, and was spit out on her chest, running down her breasts as she gasped her last breath. The video ended with Potter, covered in blood and snorting pussy juice, blood, and peanut butter from his snout, licking his lips with a nine-inch tongue, shutting the laptop and stopping the feed. I ran to the bedroom to see for myself.

Throwing open the door and ran around to her side of the bed. She was on her side and covered up to her neck by the blanket. I pulled it down, rolled her onto her back, and vomited across her desiccated body, my bile mixing with the blood and torn flesh that used to be my wife. The light flipped on in the room and I looked up to the doorway. Potter was standing inside the room, a jar of peanut butter between his hooves.

"Just so you know," he began, shutting the door behind him as he slowly approached, "she was telling the truth. Started out innocent enough. I was taking a leak one day, she saw the tip of my cock, reached down to touch it, it got hard, came out, and she just started stroking me off. Damndest thing I ever been a part of, but I can't complain. Felt good. Then, after a bit, she wanted to touch it more, to taste it, to feel it inside her. She liked it. Got off easy enough. Wanted it all the time. No one's fault really, well, maybe yours, I guess. Maybe."

I was no longer seeing or hearing clearly. I felt the blood rush from my head, and the room began to spin. I sat down on the floor, my hands covered in my wife's blood.

"That thing tonight, though, man, that was a doozy. Shit got out of hand, what can I say? I'm sorry about that one. Peanut butter drives me bat shit crazy. So, yeah, sorry."

"Sorry," I croaked from the floor, my mouth dry, my heart in my ears as the blood swirled all around me.

"Yeah, I carried her back in here, covered her up and woke you. Wanted to break it to you gently, ya know. Not like some mook."

"You killed her."

"About that, yeah. Well, you know the sayin, 'kill one, you might as well kill em all?' Or some shit like that."

"What?"

He unscrewed the peanut butter. "Take a deep breath, this is going to sting a little."

WARE THE DEEP

STEPHANIE PARK

NIGHT COMES LATE IN MAY. The heavens turn toward summer, and, in the northern states, the sun often sets past nine o'clock. But night still comes cold at times, and Zachary's breath steamed as he trotted through the woods, the sunset's ruddy glow lingering in the sky above.

He was a wolf, at least for now; loping easily between the pines, ferns, and mosses of Washington's coastal forest. This land was lush and wet, a temperate rainforest where it rained or snowed more often than anywhere else in the country. Though the terrain suited his kind, Zachary was alone. There were no native wolves living among these trees; the state's few packs lived to the east, far from civilization. Here, though, civilization was quite near at hand.

Ahead of Zachary, lights burned, filtering through the trees, and his amber eyes flashed green as they caught the lamps of a little coastal village.

He paused, just within the shelter of the trees, and wiggled out of a small bundle he'd borne on his back. As if trying to get a better view of the town, he reared up on his hind legs. But this motion continued far past the normal reach of a wolf as his flesh shifted and flowed unnaturally, his bones twisting and bending. For a moment, the motions paused, and a wolf-man, humanoid in outline, but still canine in nature, leered with lolling tongue at the town spread out before him. Then the change continued, and a man stood naked in the cold night air. He was tall, his tanned body outlined in hard-won muscle. His hair was dark, just long enough to be shaggy, and his eyes shared their striking amber with the wolf who had stood there moments before.

He bent and picked up the bundle he'd tied to his back some hours previous. It unfolded to reveal jeans, a shirt, and a hoodie, all folded around shoes and socks.

Clothed, Zachary walked out of the woods and into town.

Travel guides called it "sleepy" and "quaint." Tourists swelled its streets in high summer, but for now it was mostly quiet after dark. A neon sign caught the werewolf's eye and he smiled. Towns like this might be half-dead this time of year, but there was always at least one bar still open. He headed toward it, feeling the thrill of the hunt stir in his chest. Perhaps it would come to naught, but perhaps he might find the prey he sought there.

Inside, the bar was nearly empty. It was late on a weeknight, so Zachary wasn't that surprised. He was about to turn and head for the woods when he noticed the woman sitting alone at the bar proper. He straightened, and one corner of his mouth twitched up in a predatory smile. Perfect. As casual as could be, he padded across the room and seated himself at the bar stool next to her. She looked over at him curiously, no doubt giving him a once over, as he did the same to her.

She was tall, nearly as tall as him, and a little bit on the pudgy side. Not fat by any measure, but she carried a bit of bulk around her waist. Her skin was pale, and looked just a little bit unhealthy, as if she'd been recently sick. Her hair was a light blonde: almost white, falling just past her ears in lank, unwashed lines. Her eyes, however, stood in stark contrast to her pale appearance: they were jet black, hard to read and seemed hardly to move, even when she looked across at him. She was dressed simply, in jeans and a t-shirt.

Zachary couldn't keep his smile from widening. She was perfect. Slightly unattractive women tended to be uncertain, and eager for male attention. Exactly the sort of prey he was after. He felt his dick give a little twitch at the thought of what he was going to do to her.

Not yet, though. He would take his time. First off, he needed to be sure she wouldn't be missed. If she was just another tourist, she'd be his. If she was a local, he might or might not take her.

"Hello there."

She gave him a fleeting smile that showed extremely even, small, white teeth. "Hi. You new in town?"

"Just passing through." He smiled back, putting as much warmth into it as he could. "What about you? You from around here?"

"No, I'm pretty far from home."

"Oh? Where's home?"

"The Atlantic." There was that smile again, brief, showing teeth that were just a little too white. Did she bleach them? Nothing about her suggested any particular vanity, but maybe she did. Her lips were thin and pale, her mouth a little too wide, even her chin barely stood out from her jawline. *Definitely an ugly duckling,* he thought. *But no turning into a swan for her, oh no. This duck is going to be dinner.* He almost licked his lips. God, he was looking forward to this.

The bartender appeared and Zachary ordered a beer. The girl ordered a whiskey sour, to go with the empty tumbler at her elbow, and watched with interest as the bartender made it. Zachary took a swig of his beer, then turned his attention back to the girl.

"So what brings you to the other coast?"

She gave a little shrug and took a sip of her drink. "I guess you could say I'm visiting distant relatives."

"A family reunion?" he asked, hoping the answer would be no.

"Nothing so formal. They don't even know I'm coming. I just thought a change of scenery might be nice."

Perfect. "I see. It's good to travel, see a bit of the world."

"Sure is. I'm looking forward to going down the coast tomorrow. Visit the aquarium, look at all the little fishes, that kind of thing." She smiled to herself, giving another hint of those pale little teeth.

"You like animals, then?" He bit his tongue on the impulse to give a cheesy pickup line about being a beast in bed or something. She didn't seem like the type that'd work on.

"Oh, yes!" Her features were almost pretty as enthusiasm lit them up. "Especially sea creatures, and especially *sharks*. Sharks are my passion. The wolves of the sea, the rulers of a world down beneath that humans almost never visit. Do you like sharks?"

"They're okay, I guess. I can respect a predator." He grinned. "But they're basically just really big fish."

"They're not even closely related to most fish!" She sounded almost defensive, and he wanted to laugh. "They're very different. Anyway, 'fish' is so broad a category it's nearly meaningless."

"They're pretty ugly things, though."

"Predators don't need to be pretty." Another flash of teeth directed at him. "They just need to be able to hunt, and kill, and be good at it."

"I suppose that's true." Talking about predators was getting him a little too eager. His jeans felt tight, and he just wanted to jump on her, right there. If he did that, though, the bartender would have to go too; as would the couple finishing their desserts in the corner, and that would draw far too much attention.

She was still talking. "Sharks are among the oldest things still living. Sharks existed before the dinosaurs. They existed before the first amphibian crawled out of the sea. They're ancient. And Greenland sharks are the longest-lived vertebrates in the world! They can live for over five hundred years. Imagine that. There may be sharks up there in the cold dark that were alive when Columbus landed in the Americas."

"That's pretty neat, sure." He gave her an indulgent smile and a nod.

"Everybody knows about Great Whites, of course, and they are definitely fascinating creatures. I always root for the shark when I watch Jaws." She full-on grinned this time, showing short, curving canines. "Greenland sharks are just as big though, and I find them much more interesting. Not only because they're long-lived, either. There are so many other great things about them. And they're quite mysterious. For example, they're fairly slow, but they catch and eat seals. Scientists have no idea how they do that; the seals should be able to outswim them easily, but the sharks eat them anyway."

"Huh. Weird." Zachary tried not to frown. The girl had some kind of obsession, and now she was going to babble on about sharks all night and he'd never get her alone. Dammit.

"Isn't it? Sharks get weirder than that, though. Did you know that sharks are one of the few kinds of sea creature that don't release their genetic material into the sea, and let eggs and sperm get together in the water? Nope, sharks actually fuck. Violently. With lots of biting. And they're not like land animals, who can bite pretty hard without breaking skin. No, shark teeth are razor sharp. Mating almost always involves blood. Usually it's the male biting the female to hold on. Sharks don't have hands like us, after all. Female sharks survive this just fine all the time. They're hardcore." She punctuated her last word with two thumps on the bar top, the ice in her glass jingling.

Zachary felt his dick suddenly pulse. *Oh fuck yeah.* Maybe her obsession with sharks wasn't so bad after all. He was getting hot and bothered all over again. "That's something else."

"Yes, it is." She looked at him, her dark eyes bright with delight. Then she smiled again. This was a different smile. Knowing, somehow, and slightly unsettling, even for him. "But you didn't sit next to me so that I could babble on about sharks, did you?"

Now that's more like it. He tried a knowing smile of his own. "I have to confess I didn't."

"I have a hotel room down on the beach. It's maybe a quarter mile walk, and a woman really shouldn't walk alone at night. Maybe a nice, big, strong man could take pity on me and see me home?"

He blinked, thrown off balance by her sudden forwardness. But he wasn't the sort to look a gift horse in the mouth, or any other non-essential part. "Sure. You never know what kind of predators might be out there in the dark, right?"

She grinned again. "Exactly."

The girl threw back the last of her drink, and Zachary did the same for his beer.

The night had grown even colder, and seeing the girl in her t-shirt with no jacket, Zachary half expected her to snuggle up to his side as they walked. He had even started to lift his hoodie to do the gentlemanly thing. But she didn't seem to mind the cold. She walked briskly, taking long, rolling strides, though he had no trouble keeping pace. Travelling countless miles on his own four paws was a good way of keeping in shape.

As they walked, he fantasized about what he was going to do to her. First off, he'd plow her good, of course, but that was just the beginning. Looking around, he saw that the town was completely dark. The few scattered lights came from porches and bathroom windows. There would be nobody awake to hear her if she screamed.

At the pace she set, it didn't take long to reach the little beachside motel. It was the kind of dive you could find all up and down the coast; a single-story strip of basic rooms whose only attraction was the ocean view out the grimy back windows. Zachary noted with pleasure that there were no lights on in the office.

God, this night couldn't possibly go any more my way.

The girl wrestled with the ancient mechanical lock for a few moments, before shoving the door open with an audible creak. Inside, the room was clean, but more than a little worn. The carpets were threadbare and the throw over the bed was faded. All that became unimportant, however, as the door swung shut, and the girl immediately started pulling her shirt off. Zachary's eyes went a bit wide in surprise. "You're pretty eager, huh?"

"I don't see any purpose in waiting," she said, letting the shirt fall to the floor. Her eyes glanced down at his bulging jeans. "I know what you want. I know what I want too."

"Yeah, you sure do." He laughed and pulled his own shirt off, staring at the girl's body as they both stripped. The golden light of the room's dim lamps should have warmed her skin, but it was still fish-belly pale. The fat around her middle was smooth; no rolls, as she barely had a waist to speak of. Her breasts were small, scarcely standing out from her chest, and the nipples barely tinted her pallor. The fluff between her legs was sparse and as pale as her head, looking almost hairless; apparently a natural pattern, untouched by razor or wax.

He licked his lips. How she looked didn't really matter. All that mattered was what he could do to her. His dick had been ready since the bar, aching with the need to plunge into her waiting body. Beneath that, his gut ached harder at the thought of the bloody feast that would follow.

She pulled him onto the bed, and he scrambled on top of her. Her skin was cool, almost clammy. Her eyes were intense, staring into him. She was just about the weirdest damn lay he'd ever had, but at this point he was long past caring. She spread her legs for him, and he sank into her. She was wet and welcoming, but still cool, even in her depths.

Didn't matter. His cock was hot enough for both of them. He thrust hard, and grinned as she tipped her head back and moaned eagerly. What should he let her see first? A little hint of wolf in his features, a little touch of claws at her sides, maybe even a little churn inside her as his cock bulged inhumanly, and he'd see terror on her face. He'd hear moans of pleasure turn to whimpers of fear. He almost came from the thought alone but held back. He wanted, needed to savor this. Yes, it was time to change the game, time to—

The girl yanked his head down and kissed him hard, forcing her tongue into his mouth. He pushed back, asserting his dominance, driving his own tongue between her teeth.

A stab of pain made him jerk back from the kiss. She'd bitten him! His mouth filled abruptly with the taste of his own blood, far too much of it. How could she have drawn so much? He looked down at her and saw a drop dribble from his mouth to splatter on her pale, pale skin.

She grinned. Her teeth were still very white, and very even, but now they were also very, very sharp. They were like saws of bone— flat, razor-edged and needle pointed. His blood dripped from between them and stained her lips a lurid red.

With a yelp he flung himself away from her, his suddenly softening dick slipping out easily. She laughed, her mouth too wide. Her skin seemed darker, grayish; a dead-fish color. In the lamplight, it looked matte and dull, losing any healthy sheen it might have had.

"What the fuck?" He pulled back further, then yelped as he fell off the bed.

She didn't say anything. Her grin stayed fixed, but widened, spreading across her face towards her shrinking ears. He glanced down and saw the skin on her neck ripple and split; gills opening onto bone and sinew. He shuddered and started to scramble to his feet.

Before he could rise, she was off the bed, coming for him. He kicked at her, crab-walking on his butt across the floor, looking desperately for an exit. The freak-toothed girl-thing circled around to stand in front of the door, still grinning. That horrible smile had stopped spreading, but it was still utterly wrong, and still stained with his blood. He shuddered and swung his head around frantically. Gone were thoughts of shifting form, all he wanted was to escape the unnerving girl. The window! It was open and covered by a threadbare screen. He scrambled to his feet and dived for it, forcing a hole through the mesh.

Something grabbed his foot and yanked hard as he tried to climb the sill. Then there was a stab of horrible pain and he shrieked helplessly. He looked back to see the girl gripping his ankle and *biting* his foot. She let go and swallowed. Oh god. He was missing all his toes. She'd fucking bitten off his toes. He tumbled out the window, landing in the coarse grass. He tried to stand and almost collapsed as agony spiked up from his foot, blood soaking into the dry ground under him.

"Heh."

The soft sound of amusement drew his eyes up to the window. The girl was standing there, still grinning, even more of his blood not just on her teeth but all down her chin and staining her breasts. The light from the room behind her made her into a shadowy silhouette, but the dark blood still stood out in sharp contrast to her pale skin.

Zachary felt faint. He knew he was in shock from the loss of his toes. His fucking toes! What the fuck! The girl moved forward, putting her foot up on the windowsill. Shock was quickly routed by utter panic. He had to get away from her. He tried to force himself to his feet, but as soon as he tried, white fire blossomed up from below his knee and he fell again. She was crouched on the windowsill now, her eyes not moving from him as she moved slowly forward.

Oh god he had to get out of here. Throwing caution to the wind he took his wolf's form again. Four legs meant he could run with one disabled.

"Interesting," said the girl, dropping lightly down from the window. He didn't stick around to see what else she might have to say, he ran directly away from her. He was a little slower than usual with just three working legs, but he had to be faster than she was, right?

He felt grass turn to sand under his paws and skidded to a stop, realizing that in his panic he'd run right towards the ocean. The girl was some kind of fish-shark-tooth-monster-thing, so she probably would be right at home in the water. He looked back. She was too close. *Can't pause, can't go back, can't go into the water . . . fuck.* He darted to the left, along the beach, headed for what should be the downtown area of the little coastal village. The girl turned too, matching his course along the top of the beach. He couldn't cut up towards land, she'd close the angle and get him easily. He had to get a bigger lead on her. Looking back, she was just trotting along, not going all that fast. Fish were slow, right? He could just outrun her.

Somewhere in the back of his mind her heard the girl's voice saying " . . . the seals should be able to outswim them easily, but the sharks eat them anyway . . . " He shuddered and ran faster, spotting the sand behind him with blood from his paw, now missing its claws. He couldn't keep this up forever, but he had to get ahead of the girl.

He glanced to the side. She was still there, a little bit behind him, but now seaside bungalows had been replaced by a low, irregular cliff of black basalt. He snarled and kept running, dark cliffs to his left, the faintly luminescent, foaming sea to his right. Waves splashed and sucked at his paws, the beach too narrow for him to avoid the water entirely.

He'd get enough of a lead soon, and then he'd just need a break in the cliff, or a few extra moments to scramble up it. It wasn't sheer or even all that steep. It was just annoying. He could do this.

Suddenly blackness loomed out of the dark night ahead of him and he almost tumbled to a halt. A higher cliff, part of a head thrusting out into the water, rose in front of him. He looked back, certain that the girl had known and would be right on his tail, but she was gone.

He blinked. A shiver coursed over him. *Fuck*. It had been bad enough having her behind him, but now she could be anywhere. If he doubled back, she was sure to get him.

A glint of metal against the black caught his eye, and he lunged forward, feeling something like relief swell in his chest. It was the railing of a staircase that ran up the cliff, cut into the stone itself. He was up the stairs in a flash, though they took more out of him than running for his life had. The stairs twisted back and forth, letting out on a little grassy picnic area, with tables and benches scattered about.

He felt faint, and his pace out of the park was slower than it had been. Blood loss was weakening him. He wanted to curse, but a wolf's tongue wasn't suited to it. He growled instead and trotted unsteadily up the short path to the town's main street, which ran north and south, parallel to the sea. He picked south, heading downtown, away from the hotel.

If he could just get to the forest, away from the water, he would surely be safe there. He looked east, toward the woods. Houses and shops lined the street. He didn't want to slow himself, going through gardens and scrambling over fences. He'd take the first cross-street and try his luck. He looked for lighted windows and signs of life as he went. All it would take was one person willing to take pity on an injured "dog" and he might be safe. But the dark night and the sleepy town that had seemed so much in his favor had turned against him. Everyone was asleep. He couldn't even see the neon of the bar that had got him into this in the first place.

He reached the cross street, turned east and froze. *Fuck!* The girl was right there, standing under a streetlight, naked and unconcerned. She looked even less human now. Her skin was a textured gray, lighter across her stomach and chest. Her breasts had vanished. Her nose had pushed forward taking the rest of her face with it into an angular snout. Her grin was even wider, pushing well past her vanished ears, showing teeth in double rows. Her hair was gone as well, and as he watched, a tail, tipped with a sleek fin, spread smoothly out behind her.

She was also taller than she'd been, almost like she could reach up and snuff the dull orange light and leave them in darkness. She looked down at him and grinned again, her lips fading into nothing.

Zachary turned and fled, his heart hammering in his throat. His panicked flight led west down the side street, but he halted again when he saw that ahead of him was the bay, a pit of dark water cradled by basalt heads, dotted with boats and lined with piers and docks. He did *not* want to go there.

To the left: shops, no yards, no gaps in between. To the right, back the way he'd come: a warehouse, running the length of the street. Ahead, the bay. Behind, the girl-thing, moving steadily, inexorably towards him.

Fuck.

He ran toward the bay. The street led straight to one of the piers. There were boats tied up alongside it, but those would be a trap, not a refuge. His mind was a haze of fear and panic and pain, nothing more coherent than a stream of *fuck, fuck, fuck, fuck*, running through it. His paw had stopped bleeding but was still sending him cross-eyed at every step. He was panting hard, half from fear, half from exertion. He looked back again. The girl behind him didn't seem to be panting at all, even as her legs began to shrink. She just moved steadily forward, her dead black eyes fixed on him. She had changed more in those few seconds. Her arms seemed shorter, her fingers were blending into fins, and her neck slowly vanishing into her shoulders. Her mouth was impossibly wide, even more teeth joining the masses in a third row. She loomed massively, seeming twice the height she'd been under the lamppost.

Zachary whined as he backed down the road and onto the pier, claws scratching on the damp wood. His tail was tucked between his legs, his whole being filled with hopeless terror.

Her face was alien, expressionless, only that horrible grin giving a hint of what might be cold amusement at his fear. She continued to advance. Her pace was hobbled by her increasingly short legs, but it didn't matter now. There was nowhere for him to go.

He gave more and more ground, until his good hind foot suddenly slipped off the end of the pier and into space. He scrambled for purchase, legs churning, and ended up sprawled on the pier, clinging to it with his front paws while his hind legs hung over the abyss, churning at nothing.

He shifted then, resuming his human form, a naked man with his feet dangling over the water, his hands clawing at the splintered planks. "Please, don't do this," he said, and was absurdly ashamed of how he sounded, his voice now a wavering falsetto.

She gave no reply, just kept walking until she towered over him.

There was a moment of stillness. He hung off the pier, transfixed by her blank, black eyes. She loomed over him, no expression but hunger possible on her inhuman face.

Then she lunged forward, her transformation completed in the air, and a twenty-foot Greenland shark closed her teeth on Zachary's head and snatched him off the pier and into the cold black below.

THE MOLT OF A
DIMINISHING LIGHT

MICHELLE F GODDARD

BLOOD STAINED THE DOORJAMB. Ribbons of flesh, pale and curling, were trapped in the wood or lay scattered on the floor. The back of Amara's dressing gown, shredded and pink, splayed around her shoulder blades like the petals of a dianthus. Beneath the thin veneer of her skin something shimmered and flexed, but where the skin was torn, overlapping scales hardened and deepened in colour, blush to deep, dark garnet.

Amara leaned against the wall. She stared out the window to the balcony that overlooked the city, charcoal sky and slate towers melding into each other, the late autumn sun sullen as it drew near the horizon. Her eyes grew distant and dull, her breathing laboured. Another cramping wave made her cry out and she doubled over with the spasm. She shook her head slowly, pain robbing her of words, any words, even just the one. No.

A bird hopped from one foot to the other, flapping madly to balance on the balcony rail. The sound of its claws on the metal drew Amara's attention and her head jerked up to glare at it. The bird flitted to the wall near the window, clutching to the brick as it tapped an entreaty on the glass. Amara slid the window open.

"So it has begun," the bird said, the words clear to Amara, despite the accompaniment of chirps. "To leave a life, one need only shed one's skin."

It had started at dawn. Tenderness had spread throughout her body, a discomfort that had her shifting and stretching on the bed to find solace. Amara's husband had already gone, the space beside her grown cold, when the ache permeated her bones. Sleep became a gritted-teeth nightmare, the sharp bitterness of anguish drawing moans and shivers. She woke sweating and staggered into the bathroom. Not even the heat from the shower could offer comfort.

The bird flitted through the gap in the window and landed on the back of the dining room chair as the phone rang. Amara reached for it but froze when she saw her husband's name. She hugged herself and let the call go to voicemail, counting the heartbeats it took to leave the message, wondering what was said in that brief moment. What words of significance, important enough, meaningful enough to stop what was happening to her? Would they make any difference at all?

"You are not going to listen to his call?" the bird asked.

Amara scratched one shoulder blade then the other on the corner of the wall. More skin fell to the floor. The stain of blood spread. "Promises. Just more words." Amara slammed the wall leaving a perfect hand sized indent. "There was supposed to be magic in those words. Magic to keep this at bay."

Amara's hand trembled as she reached back. She closed it into a fist, yet the need to tear and scratch was too great. Moaning as her nails dug at the peeling skin, she tore a ragged strip from her shoulder blades, the papery substance powdering in her hands. Amara staggered toward a chair and eased down into it, locking her hands together as she leaned forward. "Did he lie? Does he lie now?"

The bird preened its wings before tilting its head to address the woman. It fluffed its feathers in a shrug. "Didn't you? Hiding what you are."

Amara flexed her fingers, the strength becoming more and more evident with every movement; the nails that much longer, that much sharper. "I did it for him."

"Perhaps you should ask him if he sees it that way," the bird said. It twisted its head almost all the way around to look in the direction of the front door. "He will be home." Its head sprung forward like a coil released. "Eventually."

Amara glared. The hairs on the back of her neck rose. "What are you saying?"

"He spends much time away from you. There was a time when he couldn't bear to be gone."

Amara nodded slowly. "I just have to hold on. Hold on until he comes home."

She leaned over and turned up the dial on the stereo. Amara had programmed the same song to play over and over, the sound filling the cavernous spaces of their apartment, gathering in the corners like the fluff and dust that comes from nowhere and everywhere. She did not know what had drawn her to her husband's record collection. She did not know why she had picked that particular record to play, those four young men, faces sketched in ink, a black and white collage on the album cover. She only knew when she slid her fingertips across the vinyl, the song of a love ending had to be played.

Amara stood, propping herself against the wall for a moment before shambling forward to the balcony. She opened the sliding door. The wind rushed up freeing her plastered hair from her damp skin. The overcast day had silvered the clouds to lead. The city lay below, a sequined skirt against steel taffeta, each ripple and fold mottled with the leaden colours of the setting sun. The neighbourhood spread before her, streets and parks, homes and stores; the paths that run through a life, the routine that carries you like a ribbon around the hem of your days together.

Amara remembered being held in her husband's arms as they looked out. His embrace had kept her calm, earthbound, her feet anchored to the concrete of the unfinished apartment. She had wanted this condo, the view of the sky a tribute to what she was. He had given it to her without question. All she wanted, he had given, but it still hadn't been enough. Perhaps it was naive to expect their love to last. Excitement gives way to habit. Life succumbs to rote; a task to do: unthinking, unfeeling, without awareness, following a course set by forces that cared not for the magic of love. She had seen it happen to others, but she had thought it would be different for her.

She turned away from the sky and returned to their bedroom. With a wince, she slipped her tattered dressing gown from her shoulders. Sticky blood glued the material to her tender skin, pulling on the fresh wound until it succumbed to her efforts. Amara let the gown fall to the floor, kicking the silk into a pile as she reached for another. She threw the fresh robe around her shoulders, the cool comforting against her skin.

THE MOLT OF A DIMINISHING LIGHT

Amara gazed at herself in the mirror. She swept her long hair from her face, running her fingertips along the curve of her shoulders and down her hips. Even now, pain could not diminish her beauty. The sound of wings drifted up behind her and she felt a breeze at her back "After all I did, it was not enough."

"Did you expect him to know what you have sacrificed to taste this life?" the bird said, flapping its wings to steady itself on the top of the bedroom door. "Carving out and discarding pieces of yourself, to mold yourself into this small shape?" The bird settled, tucking its wings tight to its body. "You hoped he would make it worthwhile. That he would fill the emptiness. You made room for him and left yourself nothing. Stupid girl."

Amara pulled the gown across her body. "What choice had I? To remain as I was? Alone?"

The chorus deepened; the sound reaching out to her from the other room; the words wrapped a snare around her heart. Amara marched from her bedroom. She sang; the lyrics, after so many times through the tune, coming easily to her lips. The bird followed, chirping the melody, though the sound was far too cheery and mocking.

It landed on the back of the dining room chair near the console. Tilting its head, it regarded its reflection in the dark screen of the phone that lay in the charger. "Yes. He put a light in your eyes, but now it is gone." Its own eyes glistened, two points of darkness within a puff of plumped feathers.

Amara reached for the phone, the slim tablet almost too delicate for her panicked strength. Breathing in slowly, willing her fingers to barely brush the surface, she opened the picture app. She returned to the window and held the phone up, positioning it so that the pale rays of the sun fell on her face. She pressed the button and then brought it down to look at it. She stared at the screen, turning away from the waning sun, her heart growing colder in her chest. The light in her eyes was gone.

The phone rang again. She answered before the second ring. "Kurt? When will you be home?"

"Amara, what's wrong? You don't sound right. What happened?"

"Nothing. Nothing. When?"

"Didn't you hear any of my messages?"

"No."

He growled. "Amara. What am I supposed to do if you don't listen to my messages? You would already know what time I'm coming home."

"And what time is that?"

He sighed heavily "Late."

"Again?"

"Amara. We've been through this."

"No. I don't want to hear it."

The chorus filled the room. Words hung in the air, held aloft by the winged melody, a distant, urgent message out of reach. Amara's hand closed in a spasm, ending the call, cracking the screen and splintering her image. She flung the phone across the room, not seeing where it landed before dashing to the console that housed the record player. Her hand raked the air and sent the needle skidding across the surface of the vinyl until it came to rest whispering on the dead wax near the label. "It is the music. It has cursed me. Made me weak."

"No," the bird said. "The tune merely plucked a thread from a skein already unravelling."

"When did that happen?" She bolted to stand in front of their wall of fame, as he called it. A history of their life together lay before her: the vacation shots, pictures of his family get-togethers, the scheduled portraits and, in the centre, their wedding photo. The glow in her eyes would be mistaken for the wayward flash from a camera. Amara removed the wedding photograph from its frame. Her eyes had burned so fiercely that day, almost to eclipse the diamond he had placed on her finger. But as she scanned the remaining pictures she noticed a subtle diminishing of that light.

"That magic is spent," the bird said. "It is time to go. Or do you wish to greet him as you are?"

Amara began to tear the wedding photo; first in half then in quarters, smaller and smaller. The skin in her hands grew opalescent, ribbons of new muscle throbbing underneath as she ripped, until finally the picture lay on her palm, a pile of indistinguishable sparkling squares of confetti. Amara closed her eyes, tilted her head back and poured, the bits of paper flowing into her mouth as a waterfall into a chasm, vapour curling and foaming down her cheeks.

"Is that better?" The bird asked.

"No." Amara turned to look out the window, her breath catching painfully in a throat grown far too hot. Her reflection was as transparent as the glass, as if she were already gone. "I chose wrong this time. I will find another." Her face held a sky growing dark with dusk and the tips of green trees catching the night in their leaves. She was a part of them, part of the earth and air.

A fire beat in her chest as water fell from her eyes and into her cupped hands. She saved the tears and brought them to her mouth to drink them up. "I will need all of myself," she said, as if a prayer.

With a groan that was almost a growl, she bent in two. Her teeth clenched as pain flared and ran down the length of her back. Her gaze rose upwards. The clouds called to her, the span of distance a welcoming embrace. Yet something was not quite right. She felt weighted to the floor, mired to the earth.

"I can't breathe," Amara said, her voice smoke and ash. She staggered back, the height no longer an invitation but a warning. "Something is wrong." The words brought more pain than the ache in her bones or the wild stallion racing of her heart.

"Of course," the bird said. "Did you think you could take it all back with just your tears?"

Amara grabbed for the table to steady herself, her movements savage, her legs in rebellion. She willed her strength to return; for her iron-banded power to flow, to fill her limbs, to feel the breadth of the sky under her mastery—to flex and stretch and command, to be herself again. But the fountain of her power dripped sluggish and miserly, a dribble where there should be a deluge.

"I know how to ease your way," the bird said. "A taste to grow, a taste to know. That has always been the way of your kind. The only way open to you now."

"It would take more than a taste," she said staggering from the window, and wrapping her arms around her body.

Amara convulsed, one wrenching shudder and keen canines bit into her lip filling her mouth with the tang of blood. The metallic taste was like an elixir, making her mouth water and her head weightless with drunkenness. She breathed through her nose. The smells of the city: wet tar and exhaust, restaurant grease and pet feces, drew her thoughts skyward, making her long for the clean sharp smell of ozone.

"Then, you will be bare," the bird said. "Without. Less than you were. Take what you must from him. Take it so you can survive."

Amara felt the jagged edges of the skin on her back, rippled and puckered like torn gift wrapping, as her fingers sought the present within. Smooth scales met her searching grasp. She raised her other hand toward the turntable. She picked up the needle and lowered it slowly back onto the record. She stood, swaying, almost dancing, dispersing what remnants of grace left in this fragile body as her skin flaked and fell to the floor. How poignantly the song had spoken to her, putting into words the ticking moments of her heart beating in time with the tune.

"Soon," the bird said, "you will not be able to help yourself."

Amara stared at the creature. It blinked dark eyes, the movement ponderous and penultimate. Her hand crept toward her face. She darted to the ornate mirror in the hall and spread her hands on either side. Her palms pressed against the wall, her nose so close as if to lap up her reflection, to see beyond her face with its sweat induced luminosity, past pale lips and tangled hair. A black film slid over her eyes. Amara jerked back. As she stared, her eyes went completely, utterly black, the pupil and iris, one. Peering into her own gaze she found an emptiness so deep, she had to fight to stop from falling into it.

Amara's fist flew at the mirror. Shattered glass hailed around her hand. She cupped her face. Beneath the skin a glowing universe began to flow. Burning tears etched the delicate skin as they fell. Her hand twitched in spasm, nails grown far too long now, curved claws tearing through the skin of her cheek until it hung like the shredded shell of a wasp's nest.

"How easily it can be done," the bird said.

Amara staggered back, glass crunching under her bare feet. "No," she said, the ferocity in her voice making her shiver, her mouth full of daggers. She rubbed at her face, the rosy tissue of flesh sloughing off to reveal its scaled twin beneath. Amara sucked the wound in her mouth, the blood like honey sliding down her throat.

"Good," the bird said. "You must take it all back to become yourself again. What you cast aside, what you had been. You must take back what you gave him."

THE MOLT OF A DIMINISHING LIGHT

"And what is that?" The song hit a chord colourful with tension before it slid into its dark resolution. Her head rose and she smiled. "Nothing," Amara said, the sound coming from somewhere deep in her throat, a cavernous place filled with flames.

Gliding to the liquor cabinet, she reached for a bottle with one hand as the other moved to a wineglass. Amara loosened the cork and then poured, holding it up to the light as if to see the world in a rosier hue. She set the drink down and brought her finger to her mouth. A flash and a needle fine tooth pierced the skin.

"What is it you do?" the bird asked.

"It is only a drop," Amara said. The bird ruffled its feathers and then sat still, its black eyes riveted on the tiny drop of blood suspended from the tip of her claw. The red sphere grew fat until finally it fell into the glass, disappearing beneath the surface with barely a ripple. "Can I not spare him even a drop of myself?"

The little bird flapped, this time sweeping feathers into the air. "This is folly."

Amara placed the glass on the table. She found a pen and paper and wrote the words, 'to us'. "If he drinks," she said, "he will hear you, little bird."

"What do I tell him?" the bird said, tilting its head to peer up at her.

"Whatever he can bear. If he loves me, really loves me, he will come and find me and we can be together, truly together."

Amara reached for the record, but fumbled and twitched as if her hands were made up of too many bones and joints. With a growl bubbling just below the sound of the music, she clenched her hand into a fist, curved obsidian nails pressed against the fleshy part of her palm. Amara's strength tamed, she took the vinyl in her hands.

With a jerk of her wrist, she cracked the record in half. The sound of nails grating against shiny, brittle plastic shattered the silence as her hands snapped the plastic again and again. She opened her mouth and placed the pieces upon her tongue like a communion wafer. It melted, the hissing sound of steam untimely muffled as she swallowed, tendrils of smoke escaping from the corners of her mouth.

She did not need a mirror to know the change flowing across her flesh. The skin flaked and shed, disintegrating before it hit the floor. It fell in drifts from under her robe, making the material billow around her. Her hair slid from her scalp in ribbons that coiled and swirled in the eddies of her convulsions as her bones stretched and contorted into their true cast, and nails espoused the raging fettle of talons.

The thump of distant footsteps echoed from behind the front door. "He's here," Amara said, as she fumbled with the ties of her robe. She heard a muffled clinking, the jangling of too many keys into a fist. "He's here, too early." Amara fled to the balcony and pressed herself against the brick, as the clamour of a final fumble and then the sound of a lone key sliding home into the lock drifted toward her. The front door opened.

"Amara, I'm home," her husband said. "Where are you? You sounded so strange. I thought I should come home right away. Amara!"

From the balcony, she watched him. He did not see the broken glass or the empty frames, focusing instead on the wine glass. "You really freaked me out." He tilted the bottle up and read the label. "Is this your idea of an apology?" he asked with a smile. He took the glass in his hand and swirled the wine, so much like blood, even more than he knew. He drank.

He lowered the drink to the table almost too violently, the glass chiming in protest. The bird flew through the open balcony door and once again perched on the back of the dining room chair. "Hey," Kurt said. "You're not supposed to be in here." Kurt waved his arms. "Get out. Get out."

He chased the little bird, lurching toward the balcony door as he pressed shaking fingers to his temple. The bird alighted on the rail and looked to Amara with a shivering ruffle of its feathers. Kurt blinked and shook his head, the scent of the adulterated wine wafting from between his lips as he panted. He stepped out onto the balcony. There was no place for Amara to hide.

"Kurt?" Amara said. His gaze ran up her body, garnet scales and obsidian talons flashing as her robe wafted in the evening breeze. "Kurt. Do you love me? Kurt? Tell me. Do you?"

He backed away, mouth agape, hands rising to stop her approach, horror falling like a curtain over his eyes. "What are you? Stay back." His gaze swept the silk dressing gown, travelling along the curves barely hidden underneath, but when he reached her face, her eyes, he shook his head. "Oh god. No." He turned and darted back into the apartment. "Amara!" Kurt screamed. "Amara! Where are you?"

She stalked him as he stumbled toward the console, shards of the shattered mirror lay scattered across its surface. His jagged breathing filled the silence where the song had floated. "Tell me you love me," Amara said, creeping toward him.

"What did you do to my wife?" Kurt asked. He held a piece of glass in his hand. And then he didn't.

Amara looked down. The shard of mirror glinted as she took a step back. She slowly withdrew the glass from her side, as easily as removing a thorn. Betrayal however wounded her too deeply to recover.

A chill fell over Amara. The room spun, a vortex of darkness that swallowed her. Talons raked Kurt's chest. Horror turned to shock as he fell. He had barely reached the floor, when Amara was on him.

Blood splattered the wall. Blood rushed over her hands. Blood flew into her mouth, warm and bitter. "You hurt me," Amara said, arms swinging as if threshing wheat. "You hurt me."

Kurt's eyes rolled in his head. His arms batted at her. Then they collapsed to the floor, the fingers twitching. His gaze fixed on hers. His lips moved. Amara froze. She bent closer.

"Amara?" Kurt said. "Is this you? Amara? I'm sorry, Amara. I didn't mean to hurt you."

She pulled away as his eyes closed. He had heard her. Too late. For both of them.

Amara bent lower. Her mouth closed around his neck and she drank. Her teeth sank into his flesh and she swallowed. Acrid understanding filled the emptiness within.

Taking a deep breath, she pushed out her chest, letting loose the unrealized pain in her heart 'till it burst forth just below her collar bone, an ugly bruise on her iridescent skin. A glowing, throbbing spot, it began to move, flitting up her throat, then her cheek, and disappearing at her temple. With a spark, flames in her eyes finally rekindled. They flashed, a smouldering light above a mouth pulled back in a grimace razor sharp.

Amara turned back to the view, scaled skin catching the last rays of sunset. She unfurled her leathery wings as they tore through her shoulder blades. With a scream, loss and anger making the sound brittle, she soared through the open window into the night sky.

The Victims

JAMES L. STEELE

THE DEN WAS QUIET. *Not the kind of quiet that denotes the lack of noise, but the quiet that arises from so much noise it becomes silent. To the wolves outside, that kind of silence meant stay out. They lay in various places around the den mouth, waiting for the silence to end.*

Inside, a wolf lay on her side. She was in pain, her body completely out of her control. She was used to that, but labor was a new, and entirely different, experience for her.

Her body spasmed as muscles she never knew she had flexed and pushed. She wanted to scream so hard, but nothing came out. Her entire body was involved in the effort, including her voice. The air in the den was thick with pain and discomfort.

The first little one came out gently. The female whined a little as her body prepared her for the next. She had heard from her mother that the first one was the most difficult, then it happens on its own. One after the other, the pups arrived quickly. She thought of nothing. All she could do was lie still in the dirt and let it happen.

She felt the last pup emerge. She knew it was over because her body allowed her to move. To think. She reached around, sniffed the new life, and licked them clean one by one. Before she finished, they started crawling around to her belly. She licked the pups as they went by. Their eyes were closed tight, yet somehow they knew where to go. They were clean when they no longer smelled like her and had their own scents. Her belly tingled. She lay back down, and, once again, surrendered control of her body. They suckled.

She lay still for a while, her body feeding her young, the young instinctively clinging to her for nourishment.

The surrender of her mind and body to something natural was a uniquely wonderful experience. This was a loss of control she felt safe yielding to, and she took great comfort in that. It was how it should be.

Eventually, her body told her it was time to stop. She rolled over slightly and stood up. The pups tried to hang on, but their little muzzles slipped off. They sniffed and nosed aimlessly, unsure of their surroundings. The mother stood over her young and scented them again. She knew each of them by their scents. Four females; two males.

One of them had the mark over his eye. It glowed in the darkness of the den. The mother jumped away, repulsed and horrified. The pups continued to crawl around blindly, but never strayed too far from one another. The mother whined. She wanted to growl, cry, howl, scream in grief and anger at the forces that claimed one of her pups, but she knew it would happen. It had to happen.

I'm sorry, she whispered.

There was some rabbit meat by the entrance. She walked the couple steps to it and gulped it down. One by one the pups settled down and lay still. Their first day of life, their first meal, their first scents—they were exhausted. The mother walked to them, lay beside them. Sensing the warmth, they crawled over to her belly and snuggled in. A few of them tried to suckle, and managed to get some milk, but they were too tired to eat and just curled up and slept.

The mother reached around, parted her muzzle, and picked up the pup with the mark. She set him down in front of her. He felt around for the others but found none, so he curled up with his mother's nose instead. She resented separating him from the others like this. It was one thing about her own youth she regretted most, but it couldn't be helped.

My son, she said, still shuddering from the pain and surrender of birth. Now she had the grief of a marked pup to contend with as well. My little one. It's your first day of life, but I need to tell you a story. One you'll hear a hundred times by the day you're grown.

She licked him once. He twitched, still unsure, but responding to the good feeling it gave him.

The mark above your eye. I have the same mark above mine. Hundreds of animals have it, because there is great evil in the world, my son. Terrible evil.

The pup stirred, leaned close to his mother's voice. The other pups were curled up and asleep. She didn't feel guilty keeping this one awake. He had to know from the start he was different. He had to be prepared, just as her father had prepared her.

Centuries ago, little one, this evil roamed the world. It took whoever it wanted, whenever it wanted. We were taken, forced to turn on one another, transformed into monsters. We did unspeakable things to each other and to ourselves. It was a living plague.

The forces of good did their best to keep us safe, but they were outnumbered, and evil spread faster than they could manage. Its only goal was to use life for its own pleasure. The forces of good wanted to protect life, allow it to thrive on its own, but they never succeeded in holding back the evil.

The puppy was falling asleep. She felt awful doing this, but she nudged him with her nose. He stirred. She licked his head a few times. Her father told her he had done this to her as well.

One day, we took it upon ourselves to end the terror. Our ancestors offered a deal. Some would volunteer to be vessels. One day of the year, evil would be free to inhabit any of those volunteers and . . . and play. In exchange for leaving everyone else alone.

Evil was enticed. It meant they wouldn't have to struggle to hold onto their victims. No rituals to banish them. No fighting, no seeking, no forces of good to dodge. Now their victims would be willing and would put up no fight. Nobody would try to stop them from having their way. It was too enticing to pass up.

There is a barrier between their world and ours. A day was chosen for the barrier to come down, and evil was free to play.

She licked the puppy again to make sure he was giving attention. He was still awake. She shivered and whined at what was coming next. It's his first day of life, she thought. The rest could wait. But the more she thought about where she was and everything she had been through, the more urgent the need to talk about it became.

THE VICTIMS

Someday, son, you'll ask what happens to us. You'll ask me where I go when I leave the pack once a year, and what happens to me.

She winced. She hesitated to speak it. At first, she didn't know how. Everything she had witnessed in her life seemed beyond words. The marked beasts never spoke of their experiences, even amongst one another, so to articulate this was as new and terrifying as a puppy's first scent on his first day of life.

I remember my first time. I had reached maturity earlier in the spring. My father had prepared me for the day. He told me the stories so many times I could recite them in my sleep, which was what he wanted. We left the pack days early and traveled to a meeting place. Marked wolves are the only wolves allowed to cross territories, so when other wolves scented us, they let us pass without a fight.

Along the way, we were joined by a pair of foxes, mother and daughter, both with the mark above their eyes. Then six rabbits, four deer, three more wolves: each from different packs. We traveled together. Nobody spoke. I wanted to, if only to draw attention to how unusual it was for such a group to travel together but talking seemed forbidden. We walked for many days, picking up more and more marked beasts on the way.

I remember seeing other wolf packs, fox families, squirrels in trees, owls perched on branches, watching us pass. They never said a word. They never made a sound. They just stared at us as we passed. It was unnerving enough walking beside deer and not smelling fear in their scents. Now it felt like the entire forest was watching me, saying so much with their silent stares. Again, I wanted to ask my father about it, but he had said so much already there were no words left.

Days later, we came to a large clearing late in the evening. My father told me it was mutually chosen as the local gathering. We set aside places like these all over the world. Hundreds of animals were there already. The clearing was full of wolves, bears, cougars, snakes, lizards, birds of prey, foxes, deer. Many others.

My group split up and disappeared in the massive crowd, but this wasn't like a pack, son. There was no kinship. Nobody made a noise. Nobody looked at one another. Most of the animals were looking down at the bare dirt. My father had told me nothing grew here because so much evil had touched this land. That's not what terrified me. The silence was what scared me. It was so quiet the air felt hard as stone, and my father led me right through it.

We walked by a mountain lion lying on the ground. His eyes were open. He saw me, but he said nothing. His sight was turned inward. I had never seen a cougar this close before, and I wanted to talk to him, but my father warned me not to talk to anybody, not to look at anybody. I stayed close as we moved through the crowd.

He stopped somewhere in the clearing and sat down. I sat next to him, wanting to ask so much but not willing to be the one to break the silence. So many animals here, so many species, predator and prey lying side by side, bitter enemies sharing the air without a whiff of disdain. Before we left the pack, he said when this was over I would understand why nobody spoke.

She paused for a moment. She was sure the little pup was asleep. She was about to wake him again but held her paw back instead. She realized his life was her responsibility. Her entire litter's life was on her now, and this particular pup depended solely on her to prepare him for what was to come. She now felt the weight of such a task. Waking him was unnecessary. This was rehearsal. In all the years she had lived, she had never once put into words what happened in that clearing year after year. She was now speaking for her own sake.

Our group had traveled the farthest. We were the last to arrive. I looked around at everyone. Hundreds of marked animals all sitting or lying down in the dark, staring at the ground. No sound. No noise. The trees were bare, and the wind was cold. I was shivering. I waited for my father to tell me what to do, but he only sat still, staring at his paws.

Then a single beast screamed. I looked. It was the mountain lion I passed earlier. He was up on all fours now, hunched over and turning in circles. His skin was rippling. It split open across the spine and peeled off and fell around him. He bucked and stormed through the crowd, knocking multiple animals to the dirt. He dropped to the ground and rolled. Hard. The cougar screamed and cried. I was this close to getting up and running to help, but right before I did, I noticed I was the only one watching.

While the cougar was still rolling and howling, I heard something crack. I turned and looked past my father at a badger. Another loud cracking sound came from his body, and his spine arched backwards. Another crack as his forepaw bent backwards. Multiple snaps at once and his body twisted around. If a fallen tree branch could break itself apart, it would have looked like this. Somehow the badger was still sitting upright. His bones continued to break, one by one. It happened so quickly the badger couldn't scream. I saw ribs crack and fold inward. His chest caved in, and the ribs punched through his back.

My father said are you ready?

I glared at him, then at the badger. That's when everything happened. Something swept into the clearing. The animals stirred. Some beasts were turning in circles as their flesh stretched. Bones broke and realigned and grew out of their skin. It only took a few heartbeats, and they rose to their hind paws, fur dripping in blood. They stood three times as tall, claws as long as their arms now. Their faces—Their face . . .

She whimpered and cried. She closed her eyes, forcing herself to remember for her son's sake.

They still looked like canines and rodents, cats and lizards. But huge. Bones and muscles had grown out of their bodies and they stood on bare skeletons greased in slime. Skin still covered their bodies, but their limbs were beyond it now. The smaller animals were especially grotesque.

They attacked one another. Teeth and claws raked solid bones. When they hit flesh, blood and fur rained down on everyone nearby. They devoured each other where they stood.

I turned to my father. He was gnawing on his leg. I backed away. His eyes were empty. He tore a huge strip of skin off himself and chewed it. He swallowed. I turned to run, but something stopped me.

It came into me. I felt it displacing me. Maybe it knew it was my first time. Maybe it was glad. The first thing that happened was my eyes bled. Blood . . . erupted from them. I was blind for a breath, but then I could see through the blood. I saw the spirits in the clearing. They walked among us, jumping in and out of different animals. They were laughing . . . laughing as they leapt into a few foxes, ran their bodies headlong through the clearing. They smashed their heads into a tree. The spirits left the bodies, still laughing, and flew off for new victims. Others slipped into the broken foxes. They stood the foxes up and rubbed their bodies against the trunk so hard the flesh stripped off.

She was sobbing. She reached out with her paws, scooped the little pup up, and held him gingerly. She pressed her muzzle against him, still whining, still crying.

The blood cleared from my eyes. I saw the world normally again. Pain seared up my neck. I wanted to fight back, but something was holding me still. I turned my head so I could see. A deer had her mouth on my neck. Blood poured from her jagged teeth. She was drinking my blood.

Everything in me tried to fight back. Normally I'd feel empowered to protect myself, but right now I couldn't do a thing.

The thing inside me laughed. Pain boiled on my flanks. My ribs. They had broken. They were growing. One grew out of my chest and skewered the deer under the jaw. The deer's eyes howled in pain even as its mouth sucked blood from my neck. Two more ribs grew out of me and ran the deer through her neck. She still held on.

I was moved around, taking the deer with me. My bones broke all at once. I wanted to go down and never move again, but whatever was inside me kept me upright. I had never felt that much pain before. I was bleeding from everywhere.

The bones swam under my skin and reshaped me. They didn't connect with anything. They felt like they were held in place by whatever was in me. My spine reshaped itself and lifted me upright. My limbs grew outside my body. My skin stretched to cover as much as possible, but it wasn't enough. The muscle and bone grew beyond it. I stood on my hind feet. They were just bare bones. I towered over the ground now. My forepaws were now at my sides. The deer had fallen off while I changed and was forced to look for new prey.

It made me run toward the large group of similar monsters. Beasts reshaped into whatever twisted form these things preferred, mindlessly fighting tooth and claw. I jumped into the air and landed on one wolf. I tore the muscle from her exposed bones.

The next thing I remember is standing over one of the fallen monsters. My muzzle was inside his chest. I was eating his heart. We must've fought like that for hours, for it was daylight now.

The spirits left me. My bones swam around under my skin, and I shrank to normal size, finally inside my hide again. I lay on the dirt howling. My cries joined dozens of others also lying on the ground.

Another spirit seized me, forced me to rise, and ran me headlong into the trees. I was heading straight for one. I couldn't move myself out of the way, but something else pushed me out of the way just in time as I sped by. I dashed through the forest, narrowly dodging trees and gullies. There were two of them in me. One was trying to kill me, the other was trying to preserve me. They struggled for control like puppies pulling a stick.

Maybe ten close calls later, one finally lost. I fell down a ravine. Anyone else would've blacked out, but they forced me to stay awake so I could feel every sharp rock on that cliff face. I landed in the creek below. The spirits held me underwater and drowned me. They swam me to the surface, pushed the water out of my lungs, then drowned me again. And again . . .

She shivered, disturbing the puppies by her belly. She wished this little marked one were bigger so she could hold him tighter without crushing him. She was tempted to crush him. Her little one . . . Soon to be theirs—if she allowed it.

Hours passed. Day changed to night. I must've drowned fifty times. Finally, another spirit found me and pushed the other two out. I swear I could hear them laughing at me as they left. My new host brought me out of the water. Forced me to climb a tree. I still don't know how. It took me up as high as I could go, and I jumped. It made me land on my paws. My legs broke off at the shoulders and hips.

It waited for me to suffer for a while, then it knitted my bones together and ran me headlong through the trees again, and this time I hit every single one of them. Many had bodies lying beside them. Bodies of deer, rabbits . . . Heads broken open like rotting fruit.

It took me back to the clearing. Now I saw the monsters in daylight. Elongated, muscled skeletons wearing fur and scale still fighting in this large group. I hoped I wouldn't rejoin them.

I saw a few animals breaking their own limbs and necks. They reknitted, and they did it again and again.

Others were gouging out their own eyes and eating them.

My body jerked to the side. I was walked to a fragmented skeleton of a raccoon leftover from one of those fights. It was still elongated, and the body was stretched to the breaking point. My mouth opened. I swallowed one of the bones whole. The thing inside me sped it through my intestines. It tore me apart from the inside. It made me lie still and feel everything. It wouldn't let me black out. When it finally came out . . .

She was shaking so hard the puppies were wide awake, trying to nurse again. She couldn't hold still enough to let them.

Then, slowly, I began to heal. My bones set back in place. My ruined body mended. It hurt as much as breaking it. Then I felt alone. Completely alone and in control.

I stood up. My entire body hurt. I smelled as bad as I felt. Around the clearing, the monsters that had been fighting were normal again. So many were not there. Half the animals were either dead or gone. I walked through the clearing, looking at everything. I found the cougar lying motionless on the ground. His skin was missing, and his muscles were ground up so badly he had left pieces of himself everywhere. His eyes were also gone. I shuddered to think what it must have been like, running around skinless and blind. Then I found my father.

She covered her face with a paw. The marked pup raised his blind eyes, sniffing around, feeling for his mother's warmth. Right now, she felt like she had no warmth to give.

He was in pieces! I don't know how it happened, but he had been torn apart. I didn't even have a chance to say goodbye. He warned me: now that he'd brought a child to age, they could kill him at any time, but I didn't know what he meant until then.

I refused to sleep there. I left right away. Many left with me. I ended up leading a smaller group back. They were beaten and bruised, limping. I was, too. The trip back took longer than I wanted. Nobody spoke. We shared no kinship. No joy of the pack. I didn't want to speak. It was bad enough to live it.

Other wolf packs and fox families and deer herds watched us. Silently. Now I knew why. It wasn't the silence of condemnation. It was reverence. They didn't want to put it in words either, but they knew what we endured.

She reached a paw out and pulled the little one up to her forehead. It was as close as she could be to him without hurting him. She wanted to feel his little warmth.

That was five winters ago, little one. I was tempted not to go the next fall, but that would be pointless. They will take me no matter where I am. It is their right. Marked ones travel to the meeting place so we don't hurt anyone else, and so the others don't have to see it . . . One day a year. One day a year they use us.

She clenched her eyes shut and whined as her body convulsed in fear and remorse.

I'm sorry, son! I'm so sorry! They will use you, too. In that clearing, there is no help coming. There are no limits on what they can do to you. There is no survival instinct, no self-defense. You are a plaything—a tree branch to fight over, twist and break and toss in the river—and I am so sorry!

The puppies by her belly were stirring, wiggling around. She raised her muzzle and looked down at the little marked one. Her task was to raise him. To protect him. To nurture him. Then offer him up as a sacrifice.

No, she thought. They took her father, they took her, but she would not let them take her pup.

She opened her mouth. Held her muzzle over the little one's head. She squeezed, just a little. The pup wiggled in her teeth. Just a little more pressure, and she'd spare him a lifetime of dread and suffering.

Slowly she remembered the other half of the story. The part her father always said in the most comforting voice. The part that made those reverent stares from other animals mean something.

She opened her mouth. Looked down at the little one. He curled up between her paws and tried to sleep.

I've heard stories about mankind, *she said quietly, still trying to control her breathing even as her heart raced with the memories of autumn.* They have myths of werewolves, undead creatures that feed off the blood of the living, people possessed by demonic forces. It has been so long since anyone has seen them, they think they're myths now. They have no idea who rescued them from it all.

Just before he died, my father said everything I would see in that clearing, everything that happened, everything I endured. Imagine that happening all over the world, all the time. Imagine living your entire life in fear that evil will seize you and force you to smash your head open. It doesn't happen anymore. The world is peaceful because of us. We suffer so the rest of the world can live.

Her tail wagged. She was still shaking and crying, but she had found that little feeling of warmth that gave her comfort.

My father made sure to remind me every day. We are the marked beasts. We made the contract. Because of us, the world is free to grow. Without us, little one, our civilization would never have risen. We saved them. We save all of them every year. Their silence as we pass is how they thank us.

Cries of grief and pain became cries of hope and purpose.

Son . . . Son, if anything happens to me when you come of age, please know that I didn't die needlessly. You don't suffer for nothing. Our sacrifice keeps the world going. I'll make sure you never forget.

She cradled the little one between her paws, nuzzled him, licked him gently.

Outside the den, the other wolves in the pack sensed it was safe to draw near. They scented the entrance of the den. They smelled the new life. They laughed. They played. They celebrated the end of winter and the start of a prosperous, joyful spring.

About the Contributors

Ken MacGregor (Editor) has been writing since he could hold a crayon, and getting paid for it since 2012. His work has appeared in dozens of anthologies and magazines, and the occasional podcast.

He has two story collections: *An Aberrant Mind*, and *Sex, Gore & Millipedes*. He is a board member of the Great Lakes Association of Horror Writers (GLAHW). He has also written TV commercials, sketch comedy, a music video, and a zombie movie. Recently, he co-wrote a novel (pending publication), and they are working on the sequel. He is the Managing Editor of Anthologies for LVP Publications.

When not writing, Ken drives the bookmobile for his local library. He lives with his kids, two cats, and the ashes of his wife.

Ken can be found at ken-macgregor.com. You can also connect with him via social media on Twitter, Facebook, & Pinterest

Sarah Hans (The Moon in Her Eyes): Sarah Hans is an award-winning writer, editor, and teacher whose stories have appeared in more than 30 publications, including *The Arcanist* and *Pseudopod*. You can read more of Sarah's short stories in the collection *Dead Girls Don't Love*, published by Dragon's Roost Press, or on her Patreon at https://www.patreon.com/sarahhans. You can also find her on Twitter under the handle @steampunkpanda.

Joseph Sale (Mallard's Maze): Joseph Sale is a novelist, writing coach, and student of Japanese. His first novel, *The Darkest Touch*, was published by Dark Hall Press in 2014. Since, he has authored *Seven Dark Stars, Across the Bitter Sea, Orifice, The Meaning of the Dark, Nekyia* and more. He writes for GameSpew, and has an enduring love of video-games. His short fiction has appeared most recently in *Tales from the Shadow Booth*, edited by Dan Coxon, as well as in *Idle Ink, Silver Blade, Fiction Vortex, Nonbinary Review, Edgar Allan Poet* and *Storgy Magazine*. In 2017 he was nominated for *The Guardian's* 'Not The Booker' prize.

Theordore Deadrat (Salivation): Theodore, the disgruntled spirit of a deceased rodent, was inspired to write horror by the likes of Robert W. Chambers, Laird Barron, and too many other weird fiction writers to list here. He roams the haunted backwoods of West

Virginia along with Cortez, the world's worst chihuahua. Occasionally he shares unasked-for pearls of dubious wisdom on Twitter (@Abattoirista).

N. Rose (The Hamford Pigs): N. Rose has had a fascination with the darkest forms of horror for over twenty-five years, even going so far as to write a story of one man's descent into hell at the age of twelve. He lives in Cornwall, UK, a part of the country rife with quiet lanes, secluded farms and dark hulking buildings, where it would be easy to imagine the events of "The Hamford Pigs" taking place. Find him on Facebook at https://www.facebook.com/AuthorNRose/

Paul Allih (The Willingness of Prey): Paul Allih resides in a small town in Florida where there's nothing to do but fish or develop a drug habit. When he's not writing, Paul keeps himself occupied with horror and true crime. His stories have been published by Comet Press and Infective Ink.

Rachel Lee Weist (6 Dicks): Rachel Weist resides in Eureka, California, where she lives in a one-hundred-year-old Victorian house with her husband and a host of personified animals that she calls family.

C.M. Saunders (The Others): Chris Saunders, who writes fiction as C.M. Saunders, is a freelance journalist and editor from Wales. His work has appeared in over 80 magazines, ezines and anthologies worldwide and he has held staff positions at several leading UK magazines ranging from Staff Writer to Associate Editor. His books have been both traditionally and independently published, the latest release being a collection of short fiction called *X3* on Deviant Dolls Publications.

Elliot Arthur Cross (Randall Rabbit): Elliot Arthur Cross grew up in a one-horse New England town, but now resides in a two-horse census-designated place. When not dreaming of living within walking distance of civilization, he works diligently crafting stories to help stave off his crippling college debt. He is a bad movie connoisseur, a garage enthusiast, and a cat dad.

Rue K. Poe (A Concubine for the Hive): Rue lives in Tennessee, where she co-hosts Southern Hells Podcast, a podcast created by and for misfit Southern women. She writes unusual erotic horror stories with Southern characters.

Thurston Howl (Five Nights with Teddy): Jonathan W. Thurston Howl, is the editor-in-chief of Michigan publishing house Thurston Howl Publications, is an editor for Texas press Weasel Press, a reporter for *Between the Lines,* and a graduate teaching assistant at Michigan State University. He has had erotic horror published by Black Rose Writing and Sinister Stoat Press and has appeared in myriad anthologies.

Matt Scott (Oh Piggy, My Piggy): Matt Scott is the author of over a dozen published works appearing in anthologies from Deadman's Tome, *Infernal Ink Magazine*, Horrified Press, and Whatever Our Souls. He is currently awaiting the release of his first collection, *Darkness Calling*, from Deadman's Tome. It is a volume of seventeen short horror stories. Matt lives and works in Central Indiana with his wife, Heather, and their ever-growing gaggle of farmyard friends.

Stephanie Park (Ware the Deep): Stephanie Park, who goes by S. Park (yes, you can just pronounce it "spark"), has been writing stories since she was six, when she wrote and illustrated a story about Care Bears giving each other balloons. She eventually landed in the crafting/fusuiting world, and still makes fursuits on occasion.She has finished half a dozen novels, some of which are available through small presses. Everything from serious speculative fiction to ridiculous romance. She is obsessed with vampires.She currently lives with one husband, one child, and two and a half cats, in the Pacific Northwest.

Michelle F. Goddard (Molt of a Diminishing Light): Michelle's short fiction has been published in Reality Skimming Press's *Water* anthology, and Iguana Books' *Blood is Thicker* anthology. She is also a professional musician with song credits for plays and promotional videos.

James L. Steele (The Victims): James has been published in various anthologies and magazines, including: *Solarcide, Allasso*, John Skipp's *Demons: Encounters with the Devil and His Minions, Fallen Angels*, and the *Possessed; Tall Tales with Short Cocks v.2, Bourbon Penn*, and the *Gods with Fur* anthology. His sci-fi novel *Dangerous Thoughts* is published through KTM Publishing.

www.ingramcontent.com/pod-product-compliance
Lightning Source LLC
Chambersburg PA
CBHW032014170626
46807CB00006B/2797